WRITING PERSONALS

BY THE AUTHOR OF

Out of Cleveland (stories)

Writing Personals

Lolette Kuby

ESPLANADE
Books

THE FICTION SERIES AT VÉHICULE PRESS

Published with the generous assistance of The Canada Council for
the Arts, the Canada Book Fund of the Department of Canadian
Heritage and the Société de développement des entreprises culturelles
du Québec (SODEC).

Esplanade Books editor: Andrew Steinmetz
Cover design: David Drummond
Special assistance: Leigh Kotsilidis
Set in Adobe Minion by Simon Garamond

Printed by Marquis Book Printing Inc.

LIBRARY AND ARCHIVES CANADA CATALOGUING IN PUBLICATION

Kuby, Lolette
Writing personals : a novel / Lolette Kuby.

ISBN 978-1-55065-293-2

I. Title.

PS3561.U28W75 2010   813'.54   C2010-905334-6

Published by Véhicule Press, Montréal, Québec, Canada
www.vehiculepress.com

Distribution in Canada by LitDistCo
orders@litdistco.ca

Distribution in U.S. by Independent Publishers Group
www.ipgbook.com

Printed in Canada on FSC certified paper.

This book is for
Mel
Rob
Neil
and to the memories of their mothers

Foreword

THIS BOOK PURPORTS to be fact—based on sociology, not invention, on evidence not fancy. As with all such writing, you must, good reader, analyze and question; accept nothing at face value! Wear your skepticism like a frontlet between your eyes, like a sign upon your arm. Thus you ward off cunning fabrications, the demons of deception, with which writers weave veils of illusion around you. Believe only that which can be empirically proved, and believe not that if it cannot be replicated! Then believe it only for today, for tomorrow it will be disproved.

Not that our author would intentionally deceive. Both I and her publisher, Harry of Sympler Books, vouch for her honesty, yet even given her sincere recounting of the interviews she conducts, how will she know that her subjects have not varnished their million little pieces? Is she possessed of a spiritual radar that lights up when it encounters veracity? Are facts preserved in an etheric envelope? Do odors secreted from bodies in room 810 of the Four Seasons, for example, hang in the atmosphere, so that she can pluck the true smell of the event out of the air? She will interview dozens of people. She will ask. They will answer. She enjoys none of the liberties of a writer of fiction—no omniscience, no fly on wall. She depends upon the words of others and her own inherent lie detector, which, given her trusting nature, is not acutely honed. She will have to discriminate fact from fiction. As will you.

Skeptic though I am, I am inclined to believe that people who speak about their venture into Personals, unlike scientists, bankers, lawyers, doctors, politicians, actors, etc., having no vested interest in an outcome, will tend to speak the truth. Nor will ego play a great part in their disclosures, since no one in the world except our author will know their identities. They will enjoy no public attention, not even a five second TV blip.

I also believe that those who employ Personals have a certain *joie de vivre*, a certain *je'ne sais quoi*, a certain vision of the *Comédie Humaine*, a jollity that prevents taking themselves too seriously, and people who do not take themselves too seriously are less likely to lie about themselves. (You can count that as a Gladwell hypothesis). These are individuals who are so modest, that they are able to condense themselves into five lines: "Redhead, fun-loving, reads poetry when not playing tennis, and enjoys animals more than people. Looking for like-minded mate." There she is and probably wearing the hair that nature gave her.

All right, you say. This book will be reasonably credible, but that does not mean it is the *truth*. Bravo, good reader! You have made an intelligent distinction: What is factual is not necessarily what is true. Or, even more profoundly, the truth lies not in fact. (Forgive the pun). So, come, let us reason together: This is a stone. It is what Dr. Johnson kicked to prove to Bishop Berkely that we live in a physical universe where stones are more real than ideas. This is a person; he is bilaterally symmetrical, he stands upright, head supported by neck; he speaks. He is real. He lifts his foot and kicks my behind. The pressure of his foot—the pain I feel—is real. The imprint on my buttock is real. All of that is real but it is not the truth. It is a fact about an ass and a foot—mere raw material, mere gross sensation. What is the *meaning* of the kick—to him and to me? That is what is truth. How will our author know the *meanings* of the facts she writes about—the why, the values, the causes, the motives? She will ask her subjects the what, when, how, and where of their experience. But the why is the important question. And of that, they themselves may be unaware. Ask Freud.

Finally, a note on the Gladwell hypothesis (above). It, like most hypotheses, springs from simple common sense, which we then spend the better parts of lifetimes and gazillians of dollars on "proving." There is a chance, however, that this book *may* actually prove *something*. I hope so, since the amount of time the author spends and the compensation (monetary) she derives are incommensurable.

So, onward, good reader. We will both find out what happens.

Gladwell Alcox, Esq.

December 31, 2006

CHAPTER ONE

The Writer

Wanted: One man of average height, well-muscled but not ironclad, neither overly or underly handsome, with more body hair than a baby's behind but less than a gorilla, hefty penis, good mind, good sense of humor and humoring, joyful spirit, charge not too easily discharged, for a relationship of indeterminate time with a recently divorced woman who misses it.

I AM WRITING A BOOK ABOUT the strange new world that appeared in the late twentieth century in which people look for each other by means of Personals ads. What do these ads reveal beneath the cloak of words? When do these people actually face each other, and then what? Why do they do it, aside from the obvious wish to meet someone, for whatever reason or purpose? My publisher insists that my research begin with myself, that in order to relate "intelligently and sensitively" to the experiences of others I must dip my foot into the same river. In fact he is wrong. All I have to do is *imagine* dipping my foot. I don't ascribe to the old saw about walking in someone else's moccasins. You don't have to starve to understand starving. You just have to be very hungry at 2:00 a.m. on a Sunday and find the refrigerator empty. I am, after all, a writer. Imagination is my stock-in-trade. Nevertheless to "credential" myself and please my publisher I will compose several ads using myself ostensibly as the genuine searcher.

You might think from the ad above that I intend to accentuate sex. I do not. My ads from a variety of fictitious senders will range from hot as a Caribbean *Carnivale* to temperate as a Quaker picnic—all lies, of course. But I will be scrupulously honest about my interviews with the respondents. I will not pump up the sexy parts. I myself am not very sexy. At least not on the outside. My mother cautioned me about the dire consequences of a tarnished rep from the time I was twelve, and after that, continuously, about the whole gamut of STDs and threats to my white blood count, not to mention my soul.

I plan to structure the book so that its sexiness, like mine, runs in cycles—the titillating parts to occur in clusters—say every thirty pages or so. In other words, I plan to make it easy for the reader who leafs through for the "good parts," and who becomes exasperated with authors who sneakily situate erogenous zones in symbolic table settings and landscapes. Such coyness is not fair, any more than it would be fair for a woman to slip her clitoris under her armpit, or for a man to tuck his penis away between his great and second toe. It isn't honest, and I've concluded, after many years of reflection, that honesty is the primary human virtue. (A sense of humor is second.) Besides, you can tease a lover or a reader only so much before discouragement sets in: Where is the thin line between enticement and the-hell-with-it? (Perhaps I will come across the answer in the course of writing this book. Books, you know, always educate their authors.)

Of course, I cannot guarantee that the passages that elevate levels of testosterone or estrogen will occur *precisely* every thirty pages, nor will I draw red circles around them as though they were baboons' behinds. I won't make things *that* easy for readers. Besides, my publisher would probably not allow it. It would depress sales. Why would anyone buy the book if, while still in the bookstore, one could quickly peruse the prurient parts from beginning to end?

I do want to explain that it was the publisher's idea (actually, the publisher's father's idea), not mine, to begin the book with the ad at the top of this page. "Grab 'em by the *batesem*," he said. (He's Jewish). "Sex is what sells!" Personally, I think that the sale of sex in book or flesh is not very admirable. And I definitely do not want my book to end up on a drugstore rack with a couple copulating on its cover.

CHAPTER TWO

Gladwell Alcox
(Lit. prof, Guru, Maven, and Friend)

I AM QUITE DUBIOUS ABOUT our author's proficiency as an investigative reporter. She is possessed of a nature more inclined to gullibility than skepticism, prepared to take words at face value, mistaking rhetorical patina for the color of the substance. This credulity applies particularly to men. About women she can be quite insightful. But a man with a gift of blarney could bluff her for longer than the hour or two she will spend interviewing him.

When she showed me the advertisement she intended to place, I disregarded my usual reluctance to coach or scold her and pointed out its flaws: namely, listing requirements which a respondent could not verify during a conventional interview.

"How could you determine 'joyful spirit'"? I asked her. "You would have to administer the Minneapolis Multiphasic Personality Inventory or the Millon Clinical Multiaxial Inventory.

"The requirements as to height, hursuitry, and physiognomy would be apparent, but for the concealed specifications you would have to meet in your apartment instead of a coffee shop or bar.

"Imagine, my dear what you would have to do to determine whether the man met your stated qualifications. Let us do as Einstein did when he came up with the General Theory of Relativity—a mind exercise. Imagine this scenario:

"You open your door to the man's knock: 'Hi,' he says, 'I'm Al. I called you about your ad in *The Star?*' His voice goes up as though asking a question. He's nervous.

"You invite him in with your warmest smile. 'I would like to ask you to sit down and make yourself comfortable,' you say, 'but would you mind remaining standing for a few minutes while I look you over. Would you please remove your shirt? Good. Just as my ad requests, strong arms, well-developed chest but without pectoral muscles that look like iron breasts.

"'Now, uh, what did you say your name was—Al? Would you mind removing your trousers and dropping your drawers?'

"Even if he had no objection to such invasion of privacy, his credentials might not be, what shall I say, right out front. I mean you really can't tell if an applicant qualifies if he is quite understandably embarrassed. On the other hand, an erection might indicate too little embarrassment, a kind of brutishness, a *dis*passion.

"But, let's say that he weathers the interview with flying colors yet simply does not meet the most specific of the specs. Are you to say, 'I *am* sorry, Al, but you simply won't do.'

"'Just where,' he might query, 'Just where, just how do I fail?'

"Are you to say again, 'I'm sorry, truly sorry, Al, but it simply is not broad enough by so much as two centimeters'? No, my dear, you are not one to so ruthlessly prick a man's self-esteem.

"Or, let us say that he meets all the mental and physical requirements mentioned so far. How are you to resolve the question of discharge ability? Consider, my dear, that all the other virtues are for naught if that one is lacking. It is absolutely critical, the *sine qua non*, the *ne plus ultra* . It is important in exact arithmetic proportion to the excellence of the others. You might think, no, that doesn't seem reasonable. If the person models all the other fine attributes, one can do with a little less satisfaction in this department.

"That, I dispute. Just think, my dear. If the person you are to couple with leaves you a little cold in the cerebrum; if his physique leaves a few of your chemical substances untouched; if something about his personality irritates you, then you commence the coupling with a compromise, and a further compromise is not, as your Jewish publisher would say, so *gaferlich*. But if your partner absolutely fascinates you with his mind, charms you with his spirit, and delivers every enticement to your senses, so that after an evening of dinner and dancing you are in a fine fettle of neurological circulatory and emotional readiness and you retire to someplace suitable (or unsuitable), to do it, after which you *remain* in a fine fettle, then …

"Just think, my dear. You can administer the MMPI, you can request a nude inspection, you can engage in an hour's conversation, but you simply cannot check for duration of charge by crudely copulating with every applicant.

"But suppose you are bold enough and foolish enough to do so and thus far have tried out five applicants. You find that the fifth is remarkably close to the image of perfection you have carried in your head for years. Yet, a long line of applicants is queued up outside your door as if you were a casting director, and you wonder if an even more perfect perfection could be found among them. So you try one more and then one more. And with each trial that long-ago fifth remains the most perfect. You attempt to backtrack, but he is nowhere to be found, his spoor untraceable as the snows of yesteryear, even on Google, in *temps perdu*. Or, if found again, found in the embrace of another woman, whom *he* finds quite satisfactory, in fact he can scarcely recall the sexual summons he answered so long ago.

"Think!, my dear Sylvia, before you place a Personals ad, about the ramifications, nuances, and consequences of *each word*."

CHAPTER THREE

The Writer Again

I DID AS GA ADVISED. I thought, and did not place the ad that begins this book. But I can't help but carry that ad around in my head, because it almost describes the man I am really looking for, even though that makes me feel like a predator, a stalker. Wherever I go I am looking for the one who will conform to my secret Personals ad, upon whom I will aggress, if I find him, poor innocent! There he is walking around on his sturdy legs, with his hair and his face and his penis and his good mind, walking around in the bright world of his joyful spirit, completely oblivious of this woman who is walking through the same but different world, appraising every man: too short, too fat, too serious, too dull, not this one, and not that one. Then, Oh my goodness! There he is! And she jumps on him or faints in a lump on the sidewalk so that he can't pass by without administering mouth-to-mouth resuscitation.

When I am not feeling like a predator, I'm feeling like a quality control inspector, marking "irregulars" or "seconds." Males roll down the assembly line and I stamp reject after reject. Please do not accuse me of vanity or arrogance. I know full well that these rejects are someone else's number five. I know that some of you would have written a Personals ad like this:

> Male, about five-foot-eight, built like a whippet. No bookworm. Must enjoy dancing—Rock, Soul, Bump, Salsa. Children optional. For a long-term relationship.

Or this:

> Tall, blond, Viking type. Financially secure. Sportsman and dresses like it—more Martha's Vineyard than Marlboro

Country—but must also do justice to a tuxedo. Generously appreciative of a beautiful lady.

But enough of my conjecture—side-tracking from a track scarcely begun. It just goes to show that the mind will stray at the least provocation. It will find the slightest gully in the landscape and run in it until the ground flattens out.

Perhaps the real object of my book is me. My ad should read, "Wanted: Myself." But I don't know where to look. If I were writing a memoir (terrifying thought), I would start chronologically. Not that I feel I am a chronological being. But whatever I am, it probably went through a chronological process—not in a straight horizontal or vertical line, but like the rings of an onion.

CHAPTER FOUR

And Again

So, as I said, I didn't place that first ad, but I fabricated personas in six categories: three men and three women, in three age brackets and marital backgrounds: middle-aged never married; middle-aged, formerly married; and "older." I eliminated the young singles group as being too vast a territory. There are simply too many of them; they are too flighty and they search on the Internet, not in print. I had to conscript a male friend to answer the letters from women, promising him a cut of royalties—if there are any royalties once my modest advance is paid back. My good friend Georgie is gay and would much prefer to interview the men, but he is also a keen observer of women.

I also ran a seventh, truthful ad, identifying myself as a writer gathering material for a book on Personals.

These are the ads I ran as trial balloons. I weighed every word, as I explain in brackets:

1. Older woman
It took me fifty years (She admits her age because she wants older men to respond) and three husbands (Men like women who are attractive to other men) to learn how to please a man. (I thought "please a man" was brilliant. It informs the next man that he will find her sweet or feisty, pliable or tough, sexy or tepid—anything he wishes). Recent surgical makeover took twenty years off my face. Wisdom remains intact. (i.e. the surgery removed only the wrinkles, not the brains.) If you enjoy any three of the following—dancing, golf, tennis, reading, music and art, movies, gourmet food, etcetera—please get in touch."

(Brilliant again. How many men don't like food, music, and etcetera?)

2. Older man
Still climbing hills, not over them. (He has to assure her he is not ready for the nursing home. Also that he has a sense of humor). Sixty-five years worth of vim and vigor, not to mention piss and vinegar. (Hmm. He may have too much of a sense of humor and be too hard to handle.) Generous and honorable (code for faithful and not a tightwad. What else matters? I can see female eyes light up.) No dependents. (It gets better and better; no one to come between him and his generosity.) Well-heeled. (Hundreds of female pens spring into action.) Looking for a fifty plus, (Surely some forties will take a chance on this one) well-rounded woman (Puzzling. Does he mean many interests or big breasts? Will slim, small-breasted women reply?) for fun and no games." (Ambiguous again. Does fun mean dancing or sex? Does he mean someone just to play around with? Or what? But there's still that "generous," "honorable" and "well-heeled. Worth a reply). (I'm sure I will get more responses to this ad than publishers get unsolicited manuscripts over the transom.)

3. Middle-aged woman, never married
I haven't found you across a crowded room, so I am trying the Personals. This very attractive (good), educated (This eliminates the G.E.D. aspirants), self-sufficient woman (She's not after him for his money; she has her own.) has waited for *you* for forty-five years. (Allays the guy's fear that there must be something wrong with her if she's never been married; this one is just very particular.) I hope there is a man out there (All it takes is one, and each man thinks it is him.) who is ready to settle down (uh oh, or yippee, depending upon whether the man is a couch potato or someone with gusto.) with a woman who loves sports,

horseback riding, traveling—anything from camping to bike tours to five-star hotels (That clarifies it. No couch potatoes need apply. And she clearly wants some wealth. No side-of-the-ditch camping or afternoon motels. Horses add a touch of class) to gourmet meals for cuddly nights at home. (A clincher. Food and sex.) Children welcome." (A double clincher. Greatly widens the field of applicants.)

4. Middle-aged man, never married
(This is a difficult one. Men are so much in demand that only the totally destitute, the terminally nerdy, the inextricably Oedipal, and the uncontrollably violent are left unmarried, and even those are grabbed up by women who think Stanley Kowalsky is manly). "You have been within arm's reach and yet I have not seen you. I am ready now to open my eyes and my heart. (Wow! So romantic, so willing, so obtainable. Surely I, the female reader thinks, will be the one who opens his eyes.) I am looking for a woman who is gentle yet tough, independent yet considerate, fun loving yet homey, good-looking yet not glamorous, intelligent but not pedantic, ethical but not self-righteous. (Brilliant. Every woman can fit herself into this open range, yet he eliminates the playgirl, the ugly, the clinging vine, and the stupid: She has to be intelligent enough to know what pedantic means, or to look it up. And what a fine character he must possess to not want a glamorous woman.)

5. Middle-aged woman, divorced or separated
If you do not like children (This is a serious elimination statement, especially as it starts off the ad. She's not waiting to spring the kids on him after she has aroused his interest.), if you are a player (designed to eliminate many, but the reader asks himself if flirting is 'playing'), if you need a woman to lean on, to bolster your ego, to talk to endlessly about yourself, to bring you popcorn and beer while you watch the game, you must be my former husband (She

has a sense of humor, but may be too controlling and demanding) so please do not answer this ad. But if you prize and/or have children (a good qualifier; he either has a family or would like one), if you are loyal, have healthy self-esteem, are a good listener, and pitch in to create a pleasant home (Clever, implies that men with good self-esteem are willing to hear what women have to say and to share housework), then I am waiting eagerly for your answer (Encouraging). And if you are curious-minded, full of life, established in your career, concerned about the state of the world, and spiritual (Again, brilliant. Eliminates all men except the few who possess the qualities that are really important to her, including a comfortable standard of living) just say the word and I'll rush to wherever you are. (Wonderful. She is choosy but she will really appreciate the right one and is willing to go more than half way and she won't be keeping a ledger on who contributed what to the relationship). I am forty-five and divorced for two years. (Good. Not ready to jump too soon, yet not stale on the market). I've been told that I'm very pretty (Too modest or clever to compliment her own good looks) and tall and slim enough to be a model. (That dispenses the fear that she's a fatty, while eliminating shrimps.) I enjoy doing many things and I'm willing to learn to do new things. (A nice little sexual undertone here. What 'things' does she know, what can he teach her? One worry I have about this ad is her 'spiritual' preference. Will she get answers from Born Agains, Evangelicals, and Channelers?)

6. Middle-aged man, divorced or separated
Professional Man, forty, medium build and height, back in the swim with children in tow. Steady, reliable, family man (Should I leave him sounding boring? But swim with children shows a bit of wit.) Looking for a female counterpart for long-term relationship. (That should reassure all the women who fear that they themselves are rather boring.

He's certainly not vain. Short, simple and straightforward. I'll give it a try.)

7. I placed one ad in my own identity as author, honestly explaining the purpose of gathering material for a book, a dignified ad, not a MySpace or MyFace tone of voice. I want to sound intelligent but not stuffy. Age, looks, temperament, lifestyle irrelevant, but I would like to sound important, inviting, and interesting. "If you have ever placed a Personals ad or responded to one and would be willing to share your experiences—good, bad, or ho-hum—for a ground-breaking book-in-progress with a soon-to-be-best-selling author, please write to Personals, Box 860 or call 905-886-0219. Any age, any location, any occupation, either gender. Confidentiality as complete as if I were your doctor or your lawyer." (I changed that. I don't want to evoke any association with medical examinations or legal entanglements. Instead I just wrote ...) "Perfect confidentiality guaranteed in writing."

After pondering those ads and putting them through several versions, I myself felt as though real people had written them and that I knew these people. I was eager to hear the responses. I prepared myself by cogitating on many possible replies.

CHAPTER FIVE

My Publisher Approves

BEFORE PLACING THE ADS I felt I should run them by Harry. He was, after all, paying the advertising bill, an expense he couldn't reasonably expect me to subtract from my small advance. And wanting him to know how carefully I had chosen my words, I left in the parenthetical remarks, which obviously wouldn't appear in the ads.

"Very thoughtful," he says, reading for only a minute and placing the pages neatly, front and center on his desk. "These should start the ball rolling. Want to see a movie?"

I've known Harry for three years. I *know* Harry. And one of the things I know is that his curt remark was not dismissiveness, but approval. He trusted me and my writing.

"What movie?" I ask.

"Dunno," he says. "Let's just run up to the Carleton and take our chances. Whatever. They have good popcorn. And I just want to hold your hand for a couple of undemanding hours."

We select *Memento*, not really a selection, since it was the only movie among the six on the marquee that was starting in a few minutes. Never mind. Good or bad, we would have fun analyzing it afterwards, over a glass of wine.

I always like holding Harry's hand. It's not too warm, not too cold, not too moist, not too dry, not too rough, not too smooth, not too big and not too small. It's not passive and not aggressive. The movie is awful. One of those post modern, de-structured, pretentious jigsaws that keep you guessing which piece fits into which time and space slot. "Where could this style go in movie-making?" I planned to say to Harry, "after this jiggling of fragments?

Would they start making movies with some scenes upside down or sideways, like a misaligned slide show?"

But I never get the chance to ask him. After the movie Harry has to run. "Thanks for the two hour hand-holding," he says, kissing me on the cheek, near the corner of my mouth. " Now back to work."

"Thanks for the popcorn," I say.

CHAPTER SIX

First Responders

SURPRISINGLY, THE SEVENTH ad brought the first response. Turn-around time was amazingly fast—the very day the ad appeared in the *Globe and Mail*—and I was caught off guard.

When the phone rang and a man said something about the ad, I thought it was someone from Classified.

"Is there a problem with the ad?" I ask. This catches the caller off guard and he hesitates ..."I ... I don't think so. Is ... is this the person who is writing the book?"

"Oh, the *book*," I stupidly say. "Are you calling about the book?"

"Well, yes," he says. "Well, not *about* the book, exactly."

"Look," I say. "Is this a crank call?"

"No. Not at all," he says. "Can I speak to the person who is writing the book?" "Yes," I say. "I am that person. What is it you want?"

"It is not about what I want," he says. "It is about what you want. Didn't you want to talk to people about their experience with Personals ads?"

By now I had collected myself and felt like the moron I am. I had to terminate this conversation and start over with him.

"I'm sorry for the confusion," I say. "I'm right in the middle of something. May I call you back in just a few minutes?"

"No," he says, "I will call you back."

I tended the phone for the rest of the day and evening, like a lovesick kid waiting for a call from her boyfriend. He didn't call back for many days.

In the meantime, instead of waiting for the newspaper to mail the contents of my seven boxes to me, I went and picked it up. My boxes were bulging. I began immediately to respond to the responders.

CHAPTER SEVEN

Mirror, Mirror On the Wall

IN HIS POEM "To a Louse," the poet Robert Burns wishes, "Oh wad some Power the giftie gie us/To see oursels as ithers see us." I think the last persons who saw themselves as others see them were Adam and Eve after they ate the apple. Ever since then people are either Narcissus types who fall in love with their reflection in the pool and drown by jumping in after themselves, or beautiful people who look in the mirror and see Quasimodo.

I felt it was important to find out if people who placed ads were different from people who answered them, so I replied to some "real" ads published in the *Globe and Mail,* the *Toronto Star,* the *National Post,* and a couple of free regional papers. For this too I would have to enlist my friend Georgie; he would telephone the women who had included their phone numbers. If the woman requested a reply by email or mail, I would answer the ad, after which Georgie would enter the picture.
One of the female ads went this way:

> New to the area. Elegant blonde, fifty years. At ease at the head table or in a neighborhood pub. Interests include music, theater, movies, tennis. Looking for a successful, intelligent companion to show her the city. Possible long-term.

My answer was entirely business-like. I wrote that she sounded interesting (That's the first thing you say always, no matter how stupid, insipid, or obnoxious the person sounds), and that I would like to meet her. Would she send me a phone number so that I could arrange a date?

It was Georgie of course who phoned her to set up the coffee date at Starbucks. A high maintenance woman requires dinner or at least lunch. You can always tell by their rejoinder after coffee is suggested. If they hem and haw, claim that they are busy on all the suggested times, protest that they are off caffeine, you know you have to upgrade to lunch at least. I was surprised that this "elegant," "head of the table" type accepted coffee, but then George can be very charming.

Since this was the first interview—the very gateway to my book, I was up nights deliberating about whether I should keep the appointment instead of Georgie and explain the deal or whether the "bait and switch" should be performed by him. I decided on the latter and Georgie described himself to her as a bit younger than she and that he would be wearing a red boutonniere. He tried to make a date for a few days hence, but she would be out of the city and would phone when she returned.

CHAPTER EIGHT

The Unforgettable Amy

IN THE MEANTIME, I held my own first interview with a man who answered the ad from Woman Never Married. I had intended to shock him by claiming that I was not only never married, but still a virgin. I saved that pronouncement for another interview when it became very clear that he really did not want to meet a new woman. He wanted only to talk about one he had already met.

"Amy was her name. *Amie*, I called her. *Mon Amie*. How can I tell you how sweet she was? Her answer to my ad was sweet and later her body. Sweet, sweet, sweet—doughnuts, rose petal liquor, Godiva chocolate. My wife at the time was intelligent, witty, facetious and self-sufficient. Diametrical opposites.

"I do not write or answer Personals that sound like a list of body parts, so when we met for coffee neither of us knew what to expect, physiologically speaking, and I was prepared not to be disappointed if a plain woman arrived, short of actual disfigurement. I was pleasantly surprised. She was only about five-feet-two and rather plump, but her eyes were very large, luminous brown, her teeth perfect, her breasts heavy, and her buttocks, which I didn't get a glimpse of until I helped her on with her coat when we left, round and high. She was altogether pleasing."

Well, I thought, he may not write ads that sound like a list of body parts, but he certainly seems to think of women that way.

"It was winter, a cold January, but everything about that meeting was warm—warm coffee shop, just-baked doughnuts—hers covered with multicolored sprinkles, mine a French cruller—and her smile was sunny. We talked easily and steadily—movies, past vacations, the vacations we hoped to get to. No politics, no religion. No boyhoods or girlhoods, thank god. In time, I would find out more than I cared to know about her childhood, her ex, and so forth."

I know that I must resist judgments if I am to write this book fairly, but I couldn't help not liking this man. And I doubted that he would ever find out more than he cared to know.

"When we left the coffee shop she slipped her ungloved hand into mine, and I found the gesture sweet and warm. I said I would call her for lunch. Her image engaged my mind for the next three days. Then I called. I thought three days was long enough not to seem too eager, not so long as to seem too nonchalant.

"I wondered how she perceived me—how did this very tall (six-foot-three) thin man with his grey eyes, stout nose, and ready smile, register in her eyes? How did it feel to look way up at him? How did her hand feel in his—tiny in his big palm? Whatever she saw, it was satisfactory enough to warrant an enthusiastic acceptance for lunch."

I couldn't help wishing that she had not accepted an invitation to lunch from a man who talked about himself in the third person. Amy had already become his mirror.

He went on:

"Lunch, of course, disclosed much more. She had an amazingly large appetite, about which I had mixed feelings. On the one hand it showed gusto, artlessness, and sensuality that might translate into sexuality, which, I must admit here without embarrassment, I hoped would help me in that department. One is freed by freedom, constrained by constraint. On the other hand, her unselfconscious enjoyment of her food might indicate a lack of fineness, or should I say finesse, and, horrible thought, the probability of becoming fat. I wished I could see her mother, for the mother often prognosticates the daughter's future physique.

"Two days later I called for a dinner date, and again her eager acceptance assured me that however I showed up in her eyes and ears, this man appealed to her.

"I took her to an elegant restaurant that her loveliness that evening had earned."

Earned? This interview was becoming a test of how one continues, when one actively dislikes the person being interviewed.

"She wore a brown shimmering silk dress with an amber pendant that made her brown eyes seem golden and which snuggled neatly into her cleavage. Again she out-ate me. Money is no concern, but the bill was impressive. At dinner we got around to our private lives. I was in the throes of a divorce and I told her little about my marriage or my past, except that I had been married for ten years and had no children. It is a point of honor with me not to spell out the deficiencies of my women.

"She had been married for five years to a Saudi who was in the United States studying electrical engineering. How proud she had been, she tells me, sitting at the commencement proceedings watching her husband outfitted in cloak and mortarboard, bearing the colors of his field of study, receiving his doctorate degree. I could imagine how honored she would be if she were to accompany me to a historical conference at which I delivered an important paper.

"But, poor Amy. After she supported him for five years, he abandoned the Golden Goose and flew back to Saudi Arabia, Ph.D. in hand. Didn't tell her he was leaving. Only a note saying 'I will be in touch.' The official goodbye letter with deep apologies arrived about a month later. I blamed him entirely, such incivility! Yet Amy too lost a bit of standing in my regard."

He barely paused for a breath, and I thought that if all the interviewees were as loquacious as this one, the book would write itself, provided the others weren't as overstuffed with themselves.

I would be late for my meeting with Harry, and seeing me look at my watch he terminated his oration by saying, "I'm afraid I have taken up all your time. Please tell me a little about yourself."

"Oh, your story is so interesting," I cooed. I didn't know yet how to turn someone off or speed them up. And I did want to know what happened to Amy. He already had begun talking again when I said, "Please go on."

"I lived with Amy for three years, during which my divorce was finalized. Our life together was an idyll. As I say this I realize that it was also an idle. If you want to know the particulars of our cohabitation, look in any *Harlequin* romance, or even into that step above Harlequin that presumes to be literature, 'chick lit.' We laughed, we kissed in the moonlight, we played on the beach, we took long sunny vacations, preserved in many photographs, which I have kept. When I feel rejected, passed over or outsmarted, I take them out and look at them, and when I do, the monthly gratuity I have sent her since our parting contains a small bonus. Gratuities are, after all, supposed to indicate gratitude, not obligatory compensation for service badly performed. Certainly my disposition is entirely different than when I write monthly checks to my ex wife, who had rung every cent a woman who is a successful interior designer can ring out of a ten year, childless marriage to a Professor of History.

"Amy's naiveté was exasperating. She remained patient and loving when it should have become apparent that I was involved with someone else—evenings away, which expanded to periodic nights away at one conference or another, frequent non-requisite gifts of rose petal liquor and Godiva chocolates. She was, to the end, pleasing as—forgive the vulgarity—an all-day sucker. When I informed her that I was leaving, she neither clung nor yelled. Only looked up at me with those soulful, luminous gold-flecked brown eyes, with a sadness that I admit did give me a pang. If I ever were to return to a woman to finish out my days, I would probably return to her. Our dissolution was easy. She did not sue for money, as many female domestic partners do these days. However, as I mentioned, I do send her a check every month, not because I must, but out of the kindness of my heart. Guilt? No. Should one feel guilty when a pair of shoes wears out? Where is the fault in having worn one's favorite pair exclusively until they wore out?

"And I was eager to taste what the next course of my female repast would deliver. After all, I was now fifty, and neither one's appetite nor his taste buds last forever. You understand," he said, looking earnestly at me, "that I am not in search of a permanent relationship?"

His disquisition and his caveat might have angered me if I were the woman whose ad he answered, but it was perfect for my true purpose, which I now disclosed to him. He was not in the least upset by the ruse, and, in fact, he agreed to keep me apprised of his further exploits. I think it rather flattered him to be a character in a *roman a clef.*

My cell phone vibrated insistently against my hip when I got to my car. It was Gladwell saying he would be happy to entertain me with a cup of tea if I wanted to talk to him about the book.

CHAPTER NINE

The Writer

I WONDER ABOUT THE DEMOGRAPHICS of readers of sexy books. I don't think anyone really knows. Are they sex-starved individuals or sex gluttons? Young people who want to find out, or old people who want to remember? Men, who never seem to get enough, or women, who never get enough? People whose religion imposes all kinds of conditions or non-religious people with no divine prohibitions? Married people bored with lusterless nights or libertines, for whom excess is too little? Does sex really sell? I hear a booming YES. I know it sells magazines and movies and rock con-certs, but does it sell *books* whose purpose is *serious*?

I'll have to run this by Gladwell, who has a theory about everything. My own theory is that reading about sex is most fascinating to people who are not sexually satisfied (and to academics and researchers). Here's an analogy: in the story of *The Little Match Girl,* the girl is homeless and freezing to death in a doorway in her thin, ragged clothes. When she falls asleep, does she dream about the fun of ice-skating? I doubt it. She dreams of a cozy room with a blazing fire at which she warms her poor little toes and fingers. Or take Dickens' pitiful boys, listening enraptured to tales of roasted geese with crackly skin and sweet, hot plum puddings. Why, in their cold and meager poorhouse beds they must have had veritable wet dreams about muttonchops and hot toddies. But if the little match girl were actually thawing her frostbitten little digits at a real hearth in a warm room, or if little Olivers and Jo's had bellies full to bursting with kidney pie, would they be interested in reading about fireplaces and cow meat? Full, warm, and satiated, little match girl would be perfecting her embroidery skills and Jo would be practicing his Latin declensions.

If I am right about this, it would make one wonder about the true motive of researchers like Masters and Johnson (and their experimental subjects) or a psychiatrist like Wilhelm Reich. I mean, if Reich's "Orgone" techniques for disarmoring orgasmically challenged women really worked, the women should have been regularly experiencing full orgasmic orgasms and consequently lost interest in the talking cure.

But back to my book. I am rethinking this: It should wear a hundred veils and drop each one slowly. If the reader thinks there are no more titillations to come, why would he plunk down $18.95 and take it home, even though there aren't many things beside a paperback you can buy for $18.95 these days (not even a large pizza with three toppings).

CHAPTER TEN

Interview with a Personals Addict

AFTER THE "AMY" interview I made an appointment with a man named Boyd who answered the Writer ad. Truthfully, I'm more comfortable not pretending to be looking for a boyfriend.

"Wine or coffee?" he asked on the phone. "Wine," I said. "Good answer," he said, and I met him at the arranged time and place.

"There is no end to it," he says during our interview, "just as there is no end to eating or breathing. I answer Personals, place Personals, receive letters, talk on the phone, meet the 'Person,' meet her again, break off contact, sooner or later, and start the process again. I attend a support group—Personals Anonymous. Don't laugh. We meet every Wednesday night. The label is a misnomer. Makes one think there is a Twelve-step swearing-off goal. In fact, our support group helps us stay hooked by heightening our enjoyment of the addiction. We should call it 'Enablers Anonymous.' We do sometimes cry on one another's shoulders, which relieves whatever sadness might accompany losing or leaving one more Person, but for the most part we vicariously enjoy each other's intrigues and assignations."

He chuckles at his own thoughts: "No, indeed. We do not swear off Personals. They're the purveyors of zest and mystery and excitement in our lives. Do you remember how you used to feel, in high school or college, when you were dressing for a party, or the way you could barely wait to park your car and hurry toward the music and the laughter at a nightclub, not wanting to miss one beat or one glance from the opposite sex? Of course you remember. You're barely out of college now. How long?"

"Ten years," I say, omitting that was from graduate school and reluctant to divulge anything about myself. I'm the interviewer. I'm the one who asks the questions.

"Oh," he says, looking quizzically at me. "I took you for younger. Anyway, Personals does that for me, that excited anticipation. Many of us are married, but that rarely affects our Personals relationships, and vice versa. Marriage may come into play if someone is searching for a new 'only one.' Then there's guilt, especially when bed is involved. In fact (He keeps prefacing his statements with 'in fact,' which I've usually found to flag an oncoming lie)... In fact," he says, "only a few of us in the Support Group are sexual libertines. Sex isn't required to make the game exciting."

At one time, he tells me, he found his 'only one,' but that flopped, and after resuming the search, found not another 'only one' but his wife. He did not want to exchange her, but the search itself had become fascinating and he realized it was the search itself that satisfied him.

"My wife," he says, "is perfectly serviceable. More than serviceable, a gem, really. My mother used to joke, 'Of course you should wait for the one of your dreams, but get married in the meantime.' Most members of the group did not marry 'in the meantime.' They married for love. Loveless marriage is not what sends us searching ..."

I interject, "They say that men avoid marriage because they can't stand the thought of sleeping with only one woman for the rest of their lives."

He chuckles. It's a warm chuckle, deep in his throat, reaching down into his diaphragm. "I didn't say we would be *happy* having only one sexual partner for life. I said it is not multiplex sex that we addicts crave.

"What keeps us hooked," he continues, as earnestly as if he were speaking in a confessional box, "isn't sexual variety; it is person variety. The new face, the new personality, the new mannerisms, the new mind, the new view of life. Forgive the cliché, but each time I make contact with a new woman, it is like opening a new book. What book summons us to its pages for the fifth, the tenth, the one-hundredth reading?"

"The Bible," I say triumphantly. "Or an anthology of the world's great poetry."

He was ready for my answer. "What spouse is so endlessly plumbable as that?"

What a didactic, pompous, self-absorbed asshole this man is. Endlessly plumbable, for God's sake!

"The ineluctable attraction of Personals," he lectures on, "is not really the discovery of a new person. It is the discovery of oneself as a new person. My own face becomes new, my own body, my own words. As they filter through a new mind, I know myself again. My Personals escapades—do you want to call them that? —prevents me from getting stale, not because my wife is not enough for me, but because I am not enough for me.

"You should know what I mean. Why do writers write? Isn't it because they are tired of their 'real selves,' their 'real lives?' What *is* their real life? Isn't it simply the one they display most often? And what is their real self? Isn't it simply the one they display in the everyday world?"

"No!" I say, as though he was asking me a direct question and not commenting on writers in general. "I write because I enjoy it. And I write because that's the way I earn a living. And I write to interest and inform the reader." I'm embarrassed by the words coming out of my mouth, my glib response, my straight from college English Renaissance premise that the purpose of art is to educate and entertain.

He shrugs off my answer without bothering to comment. "I'm not tired of my wife," he says again. "I still like to watch her undress. I like to observe her body when she lifts her dress over her head. I like to watch her pull her nylons slowly over her legs, or bend over to shake her breasts into the cups of a bra. And I like marriage as a lifestyle—being embedded in a family—with all a family's tribal customs—the holidays and birthdays and kids' recitals and baseball games and soccer games. When a Person pulls me away from these things, I miss them.

"What I am tired of watching is myself sitting on the edge of the bed pulling on *my* socks and shoes, seeing the same old feet. I am tired of hearing myself talk to the same sets of ears—all of them, family's ears and old friends.'"

He certainly doesn't seem tired of hearing himself talk, I think. But then, I am a new set of ears.

"It seems as though I'm always saying the same thing, telling the same jokes, even when they're new things and new jokes. With a new Person my voice sounds different in my ears, and what I say sounds interesting. My jokes are funny.

While he talked, although I bristle at what he says, I can't keep my eyes off his face. I'm inclined, when someone I'm interviewing launches into a long monologue, to lower my eyes, so as not to be distracted by what is going on around us, and to pick up any nuance of a double message, looking up occasionally to catch an expression in the eyes or mouth that might contradict the words. But I can't keep my eyes off this man's face. When he stopped talking, it was as though my favorite tune had been turned off. This was bad. This attraction was very bad. This was not the way a journalist should feel during an interview—both antagonistic and mesmerized. I was not supposed to swallow the stories whole. People lie, people exaggerate, people show-off their conquests, their brains, even their idiosyncrasies. This man was probably a boor at home. He probably hadn't looked at his wife undressing for years. He probably ignored his kid's baseball games and attended family gatherings only on the end of a leash. Wasn't all he said just a melodramatic escape from plain old boredom? But listen to that voice, the rich, resonant hum of it. Look at his eyes—gorgeous green and large, too beautiful for a man. Look at his teeth, strong and white and he didn't smile much; he didn't advertise them. His smiles were wry and rare. And his forehead—brows contracting, raising, smoothing out—like a map of his emotions. Could all that be put on? Of course it could. He was a pro.

"Once I took an especially delightful Person to a place I love— mountains, field and stream. To me it is beautiful, even inspiring. I saw it all through her eyes in a way I couldn't possibly see it by myself. I saw her disappointment. She said it was 'pretty.' Yet her detachment made me happy. Can you understand that? She was like a child who had been told a myth about a great whale and taken to Sea World sees it only as a very big fish.

"So, like all addictions, once you're hooked it's hard to stop. I'll probably be doing Personals when I'm an old doddering man. Even though it is dangerous."

"Dangerous?" I query. "You don't sound at all afraid. What are you afraid of?"

"Of being seen. Of getting in too deep. I'm afraid of hurting the Person. That bothers me more than you might think. And I'm afraid of contracting a disease—because occasionally as I said, there is sex."

We sat in the cozy velvet settee of an expensive hotel bar. A diffident waiter, whom I caught in peripheral vision, stalked our tiny table for evidence of our need for a second round. But the gilded rims of our wine glasses had barely touched our lips. Throughout his dissertation he had leaned intently toward me—no sprawl, no casual arm thrown over the back of his chair. No self-enclosing crossed arms. He was intense. Forthcoming.

Then, abruptly, with a "Shit!" and a "Sorry!" he jumps up, squeezes a bill into the waiter's hand, and says "I'm very late." And is gone.

The room collapses. My lungs collapse. But I have his phone number. I have your number, I say to myself. I also have his box number. And now I sip my drink, addled and thinking about how I would fit all this into my book. Then I sip his drink. I am still sipping and prepared to lay out another $20 for a third drink when my hip vibrates with my cell phone.

CHAPTER ELEVEN

Meet Georgie

THE CALL WAS FROM GEORGIE, asking me to meet him for a glass of wine so he could tell me about his first interview, but I was wined out and sleepy and he agreed to wait a couple of hours and come over to my apartment instead.

I left my meeting with 'Addict' hoping somehow to observe his support group. But how? If I phoned him and asked outright, I'm sure he would refuse. I might be more persuasive at a second meeting with him. Would he agree to a second interview? I didn't think so. I felt he had told me all he wanted to tell me, without getting too ... personal.

Could I possibly find that support group on my own? How many could there be in the Toronto area? I would place an ad saying "Experienced Personals user wishes to share delicious experiences with others." If he saw that ad would he smell a rat? It seemed to me very important to infiltrate that support group, where I would learn things I couldn't learn either as a writer or as a Personals user. When I got home I took a nap to sleep off my alcoholic fuzziness. Georgie rang the bell at 6:00.

About George: He is 28, looks 21, is handsome (not cute), tall (but not so tall that you hear his heart beat or his stomach gurgle when you dance with him), muscled (compact, not bulging), and he makes his living by picking up odd assignments (like my Personals interviewing), which give him a range of experiences, information, and knowledge, not to mention friends, that one rarely finds in one individual, especially in this era of specialization. He is also kind, ethical and intelligent. In a word, any woman would find him the perfect man, except that he is gay.

I think I've figured out why the best-looking, best-dressed, best-built men are gay. (I have to ask Georgie the nuances of the appellations gay, fag, faggot, fruit, homosexual, queen, and queer. In Yiddish it's *fagele*, little bird, which is rather sweet, except it implies easily crushed, like 'chick' does for females.) Probably for the same reason that women wear makeup and balance on stiletto heels and go under the surgeon's knife. Both genders have to look good to be objects of desire for men. Women, on the other hand, place looks low on the scale of desirability. For money and power they'll forgive Henry VIII his belly and Quasimodo his hump.

Georgie had redone my apartment last year and when he entered he looked around approvingly. I also approved the creamy white walls, golden oak floors, pale beige wool seating in a semicircle arrangement that allowed six to sit comfortably talking to everyone else or to the one sitting next to them, or to gaze into the white stone fireplace. Not a knickknack or a pattern around. Relief from the near monochrome came from flowers, plants, one Kandinsky and one Renoir, good enough reproductions to cost me as much as the Corian countertops. All window coverings retracted into invisibility, appearing only when the sun or the eyes of a curious neighbor invaded the premises. Georgie's dislike of fabric window treatments was enthusiastic: *Shmates* he called them—rags. (He isn't Jewish but he could access the usual list: *schmuck*—someone who is a dick, *schlemel*—doesn't know which end is up, *shlep*—verb: to carry or drag laboriously, noun: a person who drags himself along like his own package, *chutzpah*—way too audacious, *schmendrek*—his shirttail is hanging out, sometimes his nose is running, a younger *schlemel*.)

"Have a seat," Georgie says, like the apartment is his. "I'll tell you about my interview with Middle-aged divorced Alice."

"How about 'Elegant blonde'?" I ask.

"Nothing to tell. She postponed our appointment. Seems someone promised her more than lunch at their first meeting. Anyway, Alice is an interesting one."

CHAPTER TWELVE

Unwelcome Probing by Gladwell Alcox

WHEN OUR AUTHOR DROPPED in on me the other day, I inquired of her what her purpose was in writing this book. A question, as I learned, that she often asks herself, and one which every writer worth their salt, must answer. She admitted to anguishing over her conclusion.

"Glimpses. Just glimpses into an assortment of people who use Personals."

I was annoyed with her answer. "Too easy as a goal. Too loose as a concept." I rebutted impatiently, "Of what value are glimpses? You could write a book of glimpses into the lives of second grade school children, glimpses into the eating habits of pregnant women, glimpses into the toilet habits of single men, glimpses . . . ."

"That's enough, G.A.," she interrupted what could have been an endless string of examples. "Those are terrific ideas. Maybe my next book will be 'Scenes from a Toilet.'"

"Don't be sarcastic," I said. "You are obliged to give this question serious thought." I wanted to force her to articulate her purpose, however inchoate. Why Personals?

"I'll let you know," she said, closing the door behind her.

"You already know the answer," I shouted after her.

CHAPTER THIRTEEN

Harry, My Publisher

GLADWELL IRKED ME, so I went to see the person I could rely on to smooth my feathers.

Sympler Books maintains a three-room office and gives the impression of a small, old-fashioned law firm: the front office is occupied by the receptionist, who also acts as copyeditor and proofreader. Books line the walls. In Harry's office books line the walls and desk and floor. The third room is where marketing, publicity, and distribution take place—loose books and boxes of Sympler books are everywhere. I walk past the empty reception desk and into Harry's office without knocking. Harry is sitting at his desk looking more like a private detective than a publisher, a sad private detective, one who had seen too much.

His sorrowful countenance is unaccountable in someone who's had a happy childhood with wonderful parents. Or was his expression only pensiveness? Whatever it was, other women might have found it cool—mysterious and deep. But when his eyes turned to me, to me he was just my Harry. Three years ago, when my first book of poetry came out, he approached me after my reading and book signing at the pub where I was launching *Lark on a String* and asked me if by any chance I also wrote fiction.

"Hey," Harry says when I enter his office, in a tone that shows pleasant surprise, followed by a look of pleasant disbelief when I say I am just passing by and thought I'd drop in.

"Okay," I admit. "I've just come from Gladwell's and he upset me."

I had introduced Harry to Gladwell Alcox a couple of years ago and they liked and admired each other, becoming as good friends as I was with my former university prof.

"About what?"

"He asked me why I was writing this book and sneered at my answer."

"Well, why are you writing this book?"

"Let's drop it," I say. "I'll give it some thought."

He ignores my irritation and says, "Gotta run, *medaleh*. Wanna walk me to the subway station?"

"Sure," I say. I didn't ask where he was going, although I was a friend with prying privileges.

At the corner he went in one direction and I went in the other, passing a group of pre-schoolers in a line, holding each other's hands, led by one teacher and flanked by another. I turned to see if Harry would turn to look at them, as I knew he would, not realizing he would then see me turned to look at him. He grinned and gave a little shrug, as if to say, what can I do? They're so cute. I must remember to ask him about his interest in children.

CHAPTER FOURTEEN

Georgie Relates His Interview
with Alice

GEORGIE FILLS ME IN on the background: The woman who answered "Middle-aged Male, Divorced," expected her counterpart to arrive at Timothy World Coffees. The response she'd sent to the box at the *Globe and Mail* said only 'Do you want to take a chance on a cup of coffee, somewhere in the St. Clair and Avenue Road area?' Georgie had called the enclosed telephone number, leaving an equally brief message suggesting a time and place, describing himself as tall, with brown hair, and saying that he'd be wearing a navy blue turtle neck. She was to call him if the arrangements were not agreeable. Otherwise he would see her there.

Georgie continues, "I arrived at Timothy's fifteen minutes early, thinking I could settle in before she showed up. But as I soon discovered, she was already seated. At the scheduled time, a woman I hadn't taken note of rose from one of the small tables and very hesitatingly approached me.

"I'm so sorry to bother you, but is your name George, by any chance?" she stammers.

"I stood and extended my hand and greeted her with what I hoped was a reassuring smile: 'You must be Alice.'"

Georgie tells me that she suited her old-fashioned name, and when he says she was probably about in the middle of the middle-aged span, I realize that I'm not sure what middle-aged is nowadays, now that the possible life span, if not the expectation, has been extended to 120 years and octogenarians are commonplace. Does middle-aged now begin at 60? What a lovely thought. I've barely bloomed and Georgie is but a bud. Alice, he says, is nondescript in appearance and dress. I'm sure she is probably completely intimidated by finding her respondent so young and handsome.

"Yes, I'm Alice. I'm sorry, I don't know how I could have made such a mistake, but I must have written to the wrong box number. I meant to answer the ad written by a man who is middle-aged."

"I'm so sorry," I say. "You didn't make a mistake. Please give me a minute to explain."

He then confessed all (except that his role is interviewer, not writer), even his sexual orientation. This seems to immediately put her at ease: He was not a young pervert looking for an older women to ... what ... dress him in diapers?

Relieved that this was not an actual Personals date, she was very willing to tell him what she labeled as "everything" about why she was answering Personals ads.

Her marriage had been ten years happy and five years miserable, as her husband lost one job after another and slid into an impotent depression.

"I wanted a divorce for two full years before I actually divorced him," she says. "I was young then, and, what's the word in use now, hot?"

Whatever she had been then certainly did not fit the picture of what she was now, but Georgie merely says, "Well, 'hot' doesn't necessarily mean sexually eager. It could just mean very attractive or giving off a high sexual temperature."

"Well," she says, "I was sexually eager. I took up golf and the golf pro along with it, and I really wanted a divorce, but I couldn't get one."

"Because of finances?" I ask her, "or children?"

"No. Because of spiders and dark nights."

I could imagine Georgie's eyebrows lifting then contracting, his usual quizzical look.

"If I saw a spider anywhere in the house, I called Jim! Jim! at the top of my lungs until he came running and killed it."

"Lots of women are afraid of spiders," I counter. "I don't think that stops them from getting a divorce."

He is afraid he sounds argumentative, but she seems not to take offense. He's thinking that if spiders prevented divorce, lawyers would be more afraid of them than the women.

"You don't understand," she says. "I'll give you an example.

"One day, while straightening the house, picking up clothes, making the bed ... you know ... late in the afternoon because I had been on errands all morning, I saw a large spider on the wall near the ceiling. I hated spiders, no matter what their size, but if it were very small, I could brace myself and kill it with whatever was within reach—a shoe, a magazine. This one was big, about two inches, and black and furry. I simply couldn't bring myself to try to kill it ... the splatter, the mess on the wall ... and what if I just injured it and it remained there awfully wriggling, or what if I missed it and it scurried somewhere out of sight, to emerge at night, tangled in our bed clothes? No. I couldn't kill it and I couldn't let it get away."

"A dilemma," I say, mildly, though I am beginning to wonder about her mental stability. "So what did you do?"

"Without taking my eyes off the spider, I sat on the bed and watched it. I prayed for it not to move, and amazingly, it didn't move for two hours. It sat where it was and I sat where I was. You can imagine my relief when I heard the garage door open and Jim's customary 'I'm home!' Then his footsteps and, 'Ooo. That's a big one'.

"I left the room when he killed it and cleaned the goop off the wall. I had to forcibly yank my mind from visualizing the disgusting scene in order to eat dinner two hours later."

"So you couldn't get a divorce because you had a spider phobia," I sum up.

She continues defensively, "Well, spiders were a secondary fear. They don't appear that often, but darkness does and I was afraid of the dark."

"Do you want to give me another example?"

"Sure," she says.

"And while the sounds of seemingly normal people go on around us—you know ... low voices in conversations, loud voices on cell phones, hisses of the cappuccino machines, she tells me about nocturnal phobia, and I get really worried about my interviewee's stability. I didn't think you could use the testimony of nuts in your book."

"When Jim was called away on business over night," she explains, she didn't sleep at all. She kept every light in the house—

from basement to attic—turned on and every few minutes she walked from room to room checking for invaders. Each time she returned to her bedroom she looked under the bed and in the closet again: After all, the burglar, murderer, or rapist may have slipped in through the side door (carefully locked, but she knew there were ways), while she was investigating elsewhere. It didn't help that her wooded back yard backed into the wooded area of a park.

"One night she heard footsteps outside her bedroom window: A gravel path wound itself along the side of the house from front to back and the crunch of footsteps was unmistakable. They started and stopped, started and stopped. Terrified she called the police. Two cops scanned the back yard and the edge of the woods with flashlights.

"'Nothing there,' they assured her, and left.

"'But the crunch started again,'" she tells me, "'gravel moving back and forth under my window. I thought it would have been easy for 'him' to race into the woods when he heard the police car pull into my driveway, and now that they were gone, he returned. I was terrified. I could hardly dial the police number again and at the same time I was ashamed of calling again.'"

"The police arrived within minutes. This time with serious intent. They came into the house and searched each room. They searched the woods, the yard, the neighbor's yard.

"'We found your intruder,' one of them announced. 'Come out, I'll show you.'

I slipped into a raincoat and followed him to the side of the house. He shone his flashlight into the basement window well and there, peddling furiously in the gravel which had spilled off the path, staring terrified and blind into the flashlight beam, was a white opossum."

"'That must have put your mind at rest,'" I say.

"'It did for that night,' she says, 'but now I was afraid that I wouldn't be able to distinguish the scratching of an opossum from the tread of a murderer.'"

"I'm afraid to ask her if she had other phobias; after all this had little to do with Personals, but I'm curious enough to ask anyway."

"Yes, I did," she replies, apparently not worried about sounding nutty. "I was afraid of elevators and of driving across bridges. But those fears developed after my divorce. Before my marriage I was afraid of flying and of heights, but none of those fears prevented me from divorcing my husband. Only the spiders and the dark."

"So you did get a divorce," I say.

"She flashes a wonderful smile. Her first. "Yes, indeed!

"I don't know why I'm telling you all of this," she says. "I have to leave now and we haven't talked about my Personals experience yet."

I ask, "Would you be willing to meet me again? Lunch next time? Have you got over all your fears?"

"'Yes to both,' Alice smiles for a second time".

"Do you think she's a nutcake?" I ask Georgie when he finishes his account.

"I don't know, yet. Our next meeting should tell the tale. If she is, do we, I mean, you, want neurotics in the book? Would that give a true picture of Personals?"

Maybe it would give the truest picture, I say. "After all, I have answered three or four ads myself.

"Hmm," Georgie says.

CHAPTER FIFTEEN

Why I Am Writing This Book

GA's TAUNTING SHOUT at my back continued to irritate me and I determined to present him with a full written account of my reasons for writing this book, just as though I were writing a college exam for him.

There is no better way to understand our modern Western society, I wrote, than to learn how men and women find each other and form a family. Marriage is and always has been the glue of society. Every anthropologist, historian, sociologist, head of state, and clergyman agrees. Even Shakespeare agrees: the establishment of a mating pair and a promise of marriage results in a comedy, while the breach of a marital or familial bond ends in tragedy. I thought this reference to Shakespeare, taken from one of GA's own lectures, would impress and convince him.

> Professor Alcox, I am writing this book because all the old methods of meeting your mate went the way of the land phone and the girl next door. It's so much harder now to recognize what they used to call "marriageable material," for the same reason it is hard to select a cell phone: there are so many varieties and capabilities and calling plans, you can dither over a decision for a long time. I'll bet you could correlate the vigor of a society or its disintegration with the ease or difficulty of finding the right person to marry. To prove my point, I've listed eight methods of finding a mate, starting with the easiest—from the standpoint of the two people:

1. Arranged marriage. The man and woman do nothing. They do not have to know each other, let alone love each other. All arrangements are made by others. These societies are the most stable (based on divorce rate.)

2. The individuals conduct a courtship but the initial meeting is arranged by parents, and parental permission is needed to progress to nuptials.

3. Men and women meet at the homes of relatives, or else a sibling introduces a brother or sister to a friend. Or else they meet at an event, say a party, at which all the guests are members of a prescribed social circle.

4. Men and women meet at a church function. Social strata may be different, but the two practice the same life style, share the same morals, and presumably believe in the same god.

5. Men and women meet in high school. There are many more individuals to choose from here, but most occupy the same social framework.

6. Men and women meet in college. Options proliferate. So do divergent social classes, worldviews and lifestyles.

7. Men and women meet in the workplace. Not many options; most workplaces are 90 percent women or 90 percent men. There is also a strict class system within the workplace that dampens intermingling.

8. Men and women meet haphazardly, as untested, unknown, and anonymous persons in bars, nightclubs, parties. These societies are the least stable (based on divorce rate.)

But what does a person do when all of the above are gone or virtually gone—if you're not hooked up in high school or college and there are no persons of the opposite sex where you work, and you've been frustrated, disappointed, or humiliated by the bar and nightclub scene? You do what Coca Cola and Exxon-Mobile do, you advertise. AND THAT IS WHAT MY BOOK IS ABOUT. What happens to people who advertise?

Also, Professor Alcox, I need to point out to you that writing a book about Personals is not the same as writing about a fire. Or a war. Even if you're embedded with the troops. It's more like writing about the cheating that goes on in automobile garages; you have to infiltrate the territory to get the truth. You have to go incognito.

That is the information I printed out and delivered into his hands: "This explains why I am writing this book!"

He scans a couple of pages quickly and as his customary smirk spreads into a grin. I turn my back and walk out on him. I hear his laughter behind me and before the door closes all the way, I hear him say, "This is *merde*, my dear. Bring me the book. Bring me what you have been writing."

I am furious with GA. He is so supercilious, so arrogant, so insensitive, so critical!

CHAPTER SIXTEEN

Gladwell Alcox Addresses the Reader

LADIES AND GENTLEMEN. I find that I am obligated to address you directly, to apprise you of our author's true motive for writing this book, for as you may have discerned, as avid a truth-seeker as she is, she is disinclined to dig for certain self-truths.

I find her list of sociologically important issues laughable, as surely you must—a list such as a doctoral candidate might submit to a dissertation advisor for approval of a research subject: "Contemporary Alternatives to Traditional Mating Patterns." Our author did not entirely resist my suggestion that at some level she is searching for insights into herself. What writer worth that appellation would deny the urge for self-knowledge? But a more specific motive she is unwilling to explore.

In fact she is searching for love. She chose this subject because she feels particularly deficient in carrying out that search in her own name. She co-habited as though married a few years ago, unsuccessfully (about which I will inform you at a more propitious time). Before that she had fallen desperately in love three times, with men she hardly knew, starting at age fifteen: an alto sax player in a summer resort band, a medical intern, and a rabbi—fell in love the way teenagers fall in love with Ringo Star. In other words, her experience of the emotion of love remained more or less at the fifteen-year old level when she met Ted, the heartbreaking cohabitant.

She now searches among the morass of Personals to discover if, how, and why others fall in love, hoping for an open sesame, a secret door, a hidden box that contains a treasure map she can follow. Aside from the enjoyment and the edification the book may provide for *you*, good reader, her search is unnecessary, for, unknown to herself, she is already in love.

Yet, on second thought, like the universal fairy tale character who scours the world for his true home and finds it when his search returns him to his starting point, our author may require the journey.

CHAPTER SEVENTEEN

The Beautiful Woman

SHE ANSWERED THE AD by author. I was learning that responses to the author ad were the ones I most welcomed. They were less hopeful and less boring. But were their stories also less true? Were they purposely or unconsciously fictionalized or glamorized for the book? There's more than one way to make the story of your life interesting, Mr. Addict's way and the way of fantasy. Maybe neither are intended —just tricks the memory plays to liven up one's past.

But the author ad interviewees did behave differently, too. They didn't hesitate in the doorway and look around almost surreptitiously, as though hoping to spot the navy blue sweater or tweed jacket in peripheral vision before committing themselves to step in my direction. They marched boldly into the room, looked around assuredly, and headed directly toward me with hand, smile, and intention extended.

I had known by our phone conversation that this one would require lunch, and at an expensive restaurant, at that. Now she is being shown to my table by the hostess.

She is beautiful and gorgeously accoutered. Her skin is petal smooth, her straight, shoulder-length light brown hair is shiny as a nylon wig, her eyebrows are perfectly arched, her teeth ... what simile can I use for their whiteness and perfect alignment—"like a flock of shorn ewes that have come up from the washing, all of which bear twins, and not one among them is bereaved." Her clothes asserted Bergdorf's: $800 chiffon blouse, $2000 tight little summer-weight wool jacket, $1200 knee-length slim skirt. I hardly dared estimate the price of her shoes, within which, I was certain, lay exquisitely manicured toes, and heels and soles as soft as her cheeks.

I rise to greet her in my shabby suit, with a wide smile that erases the wrinkles in my upper lip, but deepens the ones around my eyes, and extend my unmanicured hand.

I order a martini, to start. She orders an Evian with lemon.

"Are you sure?" I ask.

"Yes." she says, "I don't need anything to help me talk." (Was that a slap?) "Before we start," she says, "would you please sign this? And she removes from her tiny Gucci bag a note. "I just typed this up." It merely states that our conversation will not disclose her name or, by inference or reference, anything that might identify her.

I, in turn, present her with a statement giving me the right to use her story in any medium, including book, periodical, radio, and TV, and guaranteeing her anonymity. This was one of two agreements offered to all the interviewees. The other permitted me to identify them. Few signed the latter, and I suspected the motives of those who did.

I began the interview with a probing question: "Why would anyone as lovely as you resort to Personals? You must have men dogging your trail."

"I did," she says matter of factly, "but not the kind of man I was looking for. What you are seeing is an Eliza Doolittle. I wanted a Pygmalion with power and money. Oh, I wasn't a guttersnipe. I was your average, middle-class, pretty girl, intelligent enough and with a bachelor's degree in English. That degree is one reason I consented to this interview."

I wondered instantly if I would be interviewing her or if she would be interviewing me—was she writing a book about writers? Was I the one who needed an affidavit of confidentiality?

"I answered ads in the *New York Times and* the *Wall Street Journal.* Most of them asked for a picture. I splurged on the kind of photographer that an aspiring runway model would use."

I think: She certainly seems forthcoming and not a bit embarrassed about her methods or her goals.

"I'll skip over the dregs, the lechers, and the middle incomes," she continues, "and get right to the one that matters, the one I married. I'll bet you don't find many who marry."

"Not many," I lie, unwilling to admit how few I had interviewed so far.

She tells me that before she met the men whose ads she answered she knew exactly what to expect: thinning gray hair, thickened middle, a face full of lines, pearly bonded teeth and flirtatious eyes set into a habitual come-on—the frozen mask of the womanizer. His handshake would be a bit too grasping, a bit too protracted. And she would know instinctively whether this could be the ticket to caviar, a Dior mink, an Italian villa ... for as long as it lasted.

She was wrong about everything but the 'ticket.' And it had now lasted for ten years. She had another ten to go to equal the first wife.

She had been wrong about the imagined wife too. She expected one of two types. Either a weird-looking woman with thin lips and too bright lipstick (weird because too many lifts had pulled her face up and back into a tight grimace), whose personal trainer biceps showed beneath the flesh that draped from her underarms. Or else she would be pallid, worn-out, thin-haired, thin-breasted, and beginning to be prematurely stooped.

"Terrible stereotypes," Beautiful admits. "His first wife was an attractive, graceful woman with an engaging smile. When she wasn't standing next to her husband, she wasn't walking around looking for him. And when she was standing next to him, she didn't keep her eyes pointed toward him like a compass needle. I believe she had stopped looking for or at her husband about five years earlier, when, after fifteen years, she realized that she already always knew how he would look and what he would be doing. I believe I saved her. I believe I pushed her into resuming life.

"In any case," she says, "I was not going to worry about the wife. I was not his first affair, though I hoped to be his last."

She tells me that she's sure that the wives of men who have affairs know it and either repress their knowledge to the point of mindlessness, or rationalize staying married—it's for the kids or it's for their position in society or its for his job. If those wives couldn't take care of their lives, was she obligated to take care of it for them? They both wanted the same thing—the moneyed life, pure and simple.

She and her lover met on the sly, of course, yet he contrived to get her invited to parties and fundraisers which he and his wife would attend, and he bought her tickets to concerts and plays where he and his wife would be in the audience. He enjoyed seeing her there alone, beautifully arrayed and gorgeous, just observing her and relishing the thought of their late night assignation.

As I listened to her I began to despair. How could this book be worth anything as a piece of social anthropology or psychological truth if I couldn't know when I was being lied to? All my antennae were up to detect subliminal clues to veracity and this time they seemed to be aquiver with doubt.

"Would you mind," I manage to ask, expecting her to be furious, "would you mind if I interviewed your husband?"

She bursts out laughing with a most lyrical, comforting, and sexy laugh. She didn't need the petal skin and the little lamb teeth, I thought. Her laughter was absolutely gravitational.

"All right," she says. "When would you like to do that? Would you like to come to our home?"

"Well," I hesitate, "I'd like to talk to him before you do."

That wonderful laugh rings out again. "You *are* suspicious," she says. And fetches from her Gucci a cell phone that looks like it's made of pearl. "Darling," she speaks into it, "the writer I told you I was meeting today says she would like to talk to you. Is it possible that you could find a little time this afternoon? Could she stop by your office?

"Three o'clock?" she mouths to me.

I nod.

CHAPTER EIGHTEEN

Interview with Barry (Short for Barron)
Husband of The Beautiful Woman

I TOOK A CAB TO THE ADDRESS on Bay Street that Beautiful Blythe had given me, not my usual mode of transportation. I couldn't bring myself to go from lunch at Scaramouche to a flight down dirty subway stairs and up them again at my destination to what I expected would be an elegant office.

Of course his office is elegant: magnificent view of Toronto, magnificent mahogany furniture, magnificent Persian rugs —just visualize any of the top-of-the-world offices you've seen in the movies.

The man who greets me is not exactly the "type," Beautiful had described. He's more than "thickening in the middle," in fact he's on the light side of rotund, and although his hair is thinning and gray, his eyes are not hot and hungry but (my god) sweet. The impression he gives is cherubic. But his voice is deep and resonant and rich. Anyone could fall in love with the voice alone. His voice and her laugh, I thought. What a pair. Psyche and Echo.

Even though I had raced over to preclude their collaboration in a tall tale, she could have phoned him to apprise him of what she'd told me. But I didn't think she had.

"Blythe says you wanted to get to me before she does. You don't have to worry. She is an honest person."

His version confirmed what she had told me, minus the description of his former wife and comments on the repressed awareness of betrayed spouses. He also said he was crazy about Blythe and always would be. She was The One.

I concluded that they were sharing their story just for the fun of having it in the book. It was a love story.

CHAPTER NINETEEN

Georgie's Phone Call Springs an Enormous Surprise

"YOU'RE TAKING HER OUT? On a date?"

"You can say it's partially a date, partially an interview."

"I'm amazed. First of all she is old enough to be your mother, and ..."

"Not unless she had me when she was fifteen."

"She's forty-four?"

"Alright. Nineteen."

"And secondly, she's a woman!"

"I am meeting her primarily to talk. She is going to tell me about her split from her second husband."

"How many husbands has she had?"

"Two. She's had two."

"And looking for number three."

"I don't know. She enjoys male companionship. She's intelligent, interesting and good-looking."

"Oh," I say. "I didn't know she was good-looking. You said she matched her out-dated name. What does she look like?"

"She has white hair.

"White hair?"

"Prematurely. Her face is so young you would think her hair was platinum blonde. Diane Keaton type, but bigger eyes. Alice has large hazel eyes. And I have to go. I am meeting her for a glass of wine and the next installment."

"How many installments do you think it will take?" I ask. But Georgie had already hung up.

CHAPTER TWENTY

The Dyke and the Runner

I COULD NOT POSSIBLY interview all the people seeking to extricate themselves from the slough of middle age via my mailbox at the *Globe and Mail.* I had to choose carefully, eliminating those that seemed too whacko, too dull, or too good to be true. I chose a letter that had answered 'Woman, Middle-aged, formerly married.' It was signed "Rock," and asked to meet me at Tony's Bar and Grill, "Just about any evening." The address was way at the east end of the city, near the racetrack, but the letter was ambiguous and tantalizing, so I went the day after utilizing the enclosed email address to describe myself: 5 foot six inches, hazel-green eyes, dark brown hair, slim, and (they tell me) attractive. I would be wearing (since it was Tony's Bar and Grill and not the Four Seasons), jeans, a white blouse, and a tweed jacket.

When I arrive, I am dismayed to find that "Rock," is a woman. When I tell her that I'm a writer and only wanted to interview her, she gets mad as hell and stomps out the door—unfairly I think, since her deception was at least as objectionable as mine. The door slams behind her, or would have slammed with an awful crash if it weren't on an air hinge that kept it open for a few seconds behind her furious back. I am contrite and just sit where I am and order a glass of cheap wine. The waiter opens the bottle, fills my glass to the brim, and sets the bottle on the table. Cheap was all they had.

Tony's Bar and Grill is on Queen Street and Coxwell, close enough to the racetrack to feel the vibration of hoof beats. It's one of those dingy, neighborhood bars with a neon Labatt's sign hanging in the window, dim reddish light inside, a long bar and a few tables and booths to the side of the bar and in the back. Three men and a woman sit at the bar, heads inclined at a large TV set on a shelf near the ceiling. One of the booths is occupied by a man and a woman. All the customers seem to know one another, for remarks are flung from stool to stool or booth to bar. I feel like an interloper, especially as I'm drinking wine (I should have ordered a beer) and especially because the woman who had joined me in the booth for a couple of minutes had loudly said, "I don't need this!" before storming out.

I'm not going to let embarrassment force me to leave, so I sip my wine and philosophize about clothing. As dowdy as I had felt during my interview with Beautiful Blythe at Scaramouche—conspicuously inelegant and uncool—that's how over-dressed and uncool I felt here. Cool here is a letter jacket over a T-shirt, or a wool plaid shirt under nothing, and jeans—Levi's, at best. I'm sure there wasn't a butt in the place supported by Ralph Lauren.

Mentally occupied thus, I'm not aware that the door has opened, but I notice all heads turn toward it and then slowly shift toward my booth.

"I'm sorry," she says. "Can I sit down?"

"Of course, of course," I say, displaying what I hoped was a smile duly welcoming without being phony.

"I wouldn't mind telling you my Personals story. It's just that I hate, hate, hate, being deceived."

"Like Ophelia," I say, immediately regretting the erudite reference, and feeling I must now elucidate: "Ophelia is Hamlet's girlfriend, and when he tells her that all his loving words have been lies, she says 'Then I am the more deceived,' and kills herself."

My booth companion nods as though she does indeed recall that scene from *Hamlet*.

"First," I say, "let me assure you that what you tell me is absolutely confidential—no names, no recognizable details. We'll both sign an affidavit to that effect."

"But I want you to use my name," she says. "I insist that you use my name. I'll sign an affidavit if it guarantees that you use my name."

"Use her name. Use her name," one of the guys at the bar half turns on the bar stool to coax.

We lower our voices.

She says, "That's the reason I want to tell you my story. I want you to identify me and describe my sadness, my . . . anguish. But I don't want you to name the other person. Is that possible?"

"Of course," I say. "With a writer, as with god, anything is possible."

She grins, though her eyes are serious.

"What'll you have, Rock?" the bartender calls.

"Bud and a CC," she calls back. My bottle of wine is still only one drink short of full.

"A couple of years ago, I placed an ad that basically looked for responses from lesbians—woman looking for woman, blah, blah."

I kept my face impassive, but I was startled at how quickly she offered this information.

"I arranged to meet one of the respondents here at Tony's. I was a relatively new lesbian," she says. "Before that I was married. And before that I was a singer, a café singer. I was good. A chanteuse of the down-deep-ya-gotta-know-pain-to-sing-the-blues type.

"Except for an occasional man ogling me, looking to make out, nobody listened to my songs. They all kept on talking and drinking and laughing. Once I tripped on my gown and fell spread eagle. The crowd didn't think it was an accident. They thought I was a new blues singing Victor Borge and they roared. From then on I started doing pratfalls or losing one boob out of a low-cut gown or scratching my ass with the mic, and always falling off a chair or off the stage or tripping on my dress. I was a huge success. I quit because my body took such a beating. I was black and blue all over—sprained wrists, twisted ankles. I never learned how to do a pretend fall. I wasn't a stunt man. When I fell I really fell. Same as when I fell in love."

"You found your love through a Personals ad?"

"No. Because of it but not through it. The ad turned out to be the hand of destiny.

"By the way," she extends her hand. "I'm Rock."

"I'm Sylvia," I say, "Sylvia Weisler."

"So after I stopped singing, I decided to do what I've always wanted to do—write."

Shit! I thought. Now I'll never know if she is telling the truth. Why does everyone think that if they can talk they can write? I asked if she was still writing. She nodded. Then I asked what everyone asks me, "Would I know anything you've written?"

"Not likely," she says. "I'm a specialty writer. I write porn. Not your high-class porn like what's in *Esquire*, where all the guys are tough intellectual bastards like Hemingway and Mailer. You were surprised that I know who Ophelia is." She lifts her hand to stay my polite denial. "I know because I once wrote a porn version of *Hamlet*. No death in it but the old king's. I have Claudius fucking Gertrude. I have Hamlet fucking Gertrude and Ophelia. I have Laertes fucking Ophelia. And I have Rosenbrantz and Gildenstern fucking each other. The only one who doesn't fuck anyone is the dead king. His ghost preaches puritan morality and promises hell fire to everyone else for their gluttony and salaciousness. The end, instead of everyone dying, mine is a grand saturnalia with everyone on stage fucking everyone else, even the good Horatio. I turned it into a fucking comedy," she booms, causing all heads to turn and my jaw to drop.

"But usually I just write your everyday porn, full of pussies and dongs. Like, two cars stop at a red light and the woman in one of them licks her lips around and around until they're so juicy they almost drip. He's in the car next to hers and follows until she turns into a secluded alley, where she gets into her back seat and he gets out of his car, unzipping his fly as he goes, and joins her and they do it. Then he gets back into his own car and they drive off in different directions. Or, they're in a crowded subway train and she backs up tight against him until she feels it poking her ass. Then he follows her off and they do it in a phone booth. Then he walks up 4th Street and she walks down Elm Avenue. Or they're in an elevator, just the two of them, and she unbuttons the top two buttons of her blouse and pulls out one tit. He pushes 'basement' and they do it behind the furnace. That kind of stuff. Zipless fucks, as Ms. Jong called them. Formula porn is always marketable reading. Almost no dialogue. Talking is too personal, and the thing with porn is that it has to be impersonal—just bodies. But sometimes, at the request of one of my customers, I'll slip in a real name. Kind of the written version of bedroom photography.

"The Personals ad I placed a couple of years ago—woman looking for woman—was well-written. I wanted an intelligent woman. Not necessarily well-educated, but smart and quick and curious. Not like the women in my porn stuff, who don't need a brain. I'm turned on by brains, because then you're making love to a deep well, not a shot glass.

"I waited for almost an hour for the woman who was supposed to meet me and I was about to leave when this tall, long-legged, flat-chested blonde walks in. I thought she was the one who answered my ad. Except that she looked younger than the mid-thirties her letter claimed, the rest of the description fit, and you can't tell ages nowadays, what with botox, dermabrasions, eyebrow lifts, and all. She seems very shy and self-conscious. She walks over to the bar and sits down, without looking around. I thought either she didn't see me or was afraid to come over. I call over to Ty, 'Tell the lady it's on me.' He set down her Miller's Light and a glass and says a couple of words, pointing to me. She turns only her head. Her whole body is still faced toward the bar. You would have thought her head was on a swivel, like the bobble head of George Bush by the cash register. I beckon her with my whole arm, to join me. I think she comes over because I'm the only woman in the place, for security."

"Thanks for the beer," she says, hardly lifting her eyes.

"My pleasure," I say, waiting for some sort of apology for keeping me waiting so long. I prompt her a little: "Was traffic bad or did you come by bus?"

She seems surprised. "Well, actually, I came by bus, but I got off at the wrong stop. I wanted to get off at Coxwell, then I got turned around and I've been walking for a half hour."

"Wait a minute," I say. "Aren't you _____?"

So we went on talking to straighten the whole thing out—why I was waiting and where she was headed. And an amazing thing happened to me that made my heart race and made it hard for me to breathe: I knew that this girl that I just laid eyes on would be the love of my life. Our meeting was Kismet—she got off at the wrong stop and my date didn't show up. The hand of destiny brought us together at 4:00 o'clock in the afternoon, at Tony's Bar and Grill, on October 3, in the year 2005. I wanted to jump out of the booth and pull her toward me and hold her in my arms. It didn't matter if we ever did anything else except stand there for eternity with her in my arms.

"Of course I controlled myself. She'd think I was insane if I acted like I felt. She'd be terrorized. But I was shaking inside and in a panic lest she take it in her head to get up and leave. I had to find a way to take her home with me and to keep her there forever. While I wracked my brain about how to do this, I glanced at the television set and did a double take—from the TV screen to her, from her to the TV screen, back and forth. 'Jeeze,' I practically bellow, "That's you. Isn't that you? It looks just like you!"

She looks over her shoulder, then turns back to me and says, "It's me."

It was a sportscast and she was wearing a tracksuit. "You're famous?"

"Not famous. Well, I used to be a little bit famous. I was on Canada's Olympic track team.."

Throughout Rock's tale I just kept nodding and nodding or showing appropriate facial interest. It wasn't faked. All of this was intriguing—even more gripping than Addict's support group tale. This was the sort of story that would make my book. But I needed more detail. I figured they must have become lovers, since this was Kismet, but the girl must have left, otherwise why would Rock desperately want her story and her name to appear in my book? I sat in Tony's Bar and Grill till closing time and beyond. The customers left, the Labatts sign went off. Tony said "No problem," and sat in a booth reading the paper, while Rock unfolded the rest of the story.

CHAPTER TWENTY-ONE

Rock Interview Continued

ALL THE WHILE ROCK exposed her private life to me, hoping my book would be the instrument of her reunion with her love, I felt like a trickster. Of course I would use her name as promised and instead of the usual disclaimer that any resemblance to persons living or dead was purely coincidental, I would note that the character named 'Rock' was a real woman who specifically requested that I identify her.

But I couldn't bring myself to disabuse her about the miniscule (relatively speaking) audience my book would probably have, far fewer than would read the "searching for" ad she had already run in the *Toronto Star.* She probably anticipated an enormous "community of readers," such as gathered around *The Purpose Driven Life* or *The Secret.* But what she'd get was about 2,000 readers. Maybe 3,000 if the 2,000 passed it around to friends. That is, unless Oprah somehow stumbled across the book and found it sufficiently self-helpful or spiritual.

My publisher is not Harper Collins or Random House. It is one of the hundreds of small presses in the U.S. and Canada that keep writers treading water instead of throwing in the literary towel. They have names like Origin Press, or Brandylane Publishers or Ugly Duckling or Bottom Dog Press, and they publish some of the best writing and thinking around. They're the thumb in the dike of the rising tide of cookbooks, celebrity autobiographies, and chick- or prick-lit that fills corporate bookstores. It follows that their budgets for publicists, promo, and advances could fit into your wallet. I got $5,000 and 10 percent royalties (the industry norm is 10 to 15 per cent, depending on how many books were purchased) which means that when the 2,000 first print run is sold, I will have made $4500 in royalties—not quite enough to pay back my advance.

The chance of winning Super Lotto is better than the chance that Oprah will read my book. The lottery strikes willy-nilly, whereas Oprah's crew winnows through hundreds of titles looking for the ones that tell you exactly how to become a better, more spiritual person, or how to lose weight or hang onto a husband. There's also a tiny possibility that Harry can sell the rights to a big house, provided the edition of 2,000 sells like Krispy Kremes—hot from the oven.

"Were you a lesbian when you were married?" I ask.

"I don't know if I am a les now. I think people are all naturally androgynous. Circumstances push you one way or another . . . or drag you. I was sick of men, but as to being a les, I can only say I fell more madly in love with this girl than I had ever been with a man."

"Was she a lesbian?"

"She was nothing. She was asexual. I don't think sex with a woman had ever entered her mind, but she was terrified of men."

"Why?" I ask, and construe the only reason I can think of. "Was she abused?"

"Not actually. Not physically. Only in her imagination," Rock says.

Tony had by now wiped the bar clean about twenty times, turned off the neon sign, and was sitting in a booth with his arms on the table and his head in his arms.

Rock says, "I can't keep Tony here any longer. Can we make this a serial?"

"Absolutely," I say. "When can I come again? Tomorrow?"

CHAPTER TWENTY-TWO

Author's Misgivings About the Book Again

DOUBTS ABOUT MY BOOK keep playing in the background, even though I repeatedly justify its purpose and value. What was I doing with such a trivial subject, bordering on trash? Cities were tumbling, people were starving, zealots were claiming to know exactly what God wanted, and what he wanted was for them to kill or silence everyone else, while I was writing about the lies and lecheries and inconsequential romantic monopolies of egoists. Reason came to my defense: I was writing about what people had done immemorially; they were looking for mates, companions, partners, economic security, excitement, and sex. Love too? Sure. Can you really search for love? Mustn't it just find you—across a crowded room or by moving into the house next door? But placing an advertisement—so artificial—those mini-resumes and abbreviated bios. Wasn't that a business transaction? Didn't that make you a commodity? Wouldn't the person you could love be just the one who did NOT fit the description you outlined in your ad? And wouldn't someone love you for just those qualities you couldn't label? I was tempted to answer an ad this way:

> Dear _____, I am answering your ad because I am exactly none of the things you claim to want. Why not risk it? All you could lose would be a half hour. Maybe less. I'll pay for the coffee.

CHAPTER TWENTY-THREE

The Next Day at Tony's Bar and Grill.

WHEN I ENTER, Tony greets me like I was a regular, and the regulars who had been there the night before wave and smile. Evidently, anyone Rock wanted to see again, everyone else was also happy to see.

Rock goes on to tell me what caused Tina's (that's the name I will not use when the book is published) phobic fear of men. Ironically, she says, the same cause revealed an amazing athletic ability.

"One evening, when Tina was about eleven years old, there was a movie she wanted badly to see. She and her mother usually went to the movies together when her father was out of town. This evening her mother couldn't go, and after her daughter's unrelenting pleading, she decided to let Tina go alone. The theater was at the corner of their long tree-shaded street which went down a hill, was crossed by an alleyway, and went up a hill to the main street and the movies.

"Her mother drummed her with warnings: 'Don't sit next to anyone if you can help it. If it is crowded be sure to find a seat next to a woman. If the seat next to you is empty and a man sits down, get up immediately and move to another seat. If there is no seat except next to a man, sit in the corner of your seat, as far away from him as possible. If he should put his hand on your leg, don't be ashamed to scream. You scream! When the movie is over, come directly home as quickly as you can. Hopefully, others from our street will be walking home. There's safety in numbers. If you suspect someone is following you, run to the nearest house and bang loudly on the door.'

"You can imagine," Rock says. "Tina was so filled with anxiety she hardly saw the movie. When it was over she waited under the marquee for a few minutes for possible neighbors, but as the crowd thinned out, she crossed the main street and headed home. It had been dusk when she left home; now it was pitch dark. The thick canopy of leaves made her street seem like a cave, except where a street lamp shone through the foliage, or a lighted living room window glimmered through the bushes. She hurried, half running, half walking, looking nervously to the right and left.

"At the bottom of the hill, by the alley, she saw a parked car directly under a street lamp, and as she passed it, she saw a man in the car. His pants were pulled down to his knees and a stiff penis thrust up from between his thighs. Through the partly opened window he said, 'Come here girly. I have something for you.'"

Rock had barely taken a breath during this narration and seemed as agitated as if it had happened to her.

"That's it?" I say. "That's what caused her overwhelming fear of men?" I was thinking that Tina must have a very tender psyche, indeed. "And where's the irony? The athletic prowess?"

"Well, wait," Rock says. "That's not the end of the story.

"Tina was terrified, but not petrified. She broke into a run. She ran as though her life depended on it. She covered the distance from the alley to home—about a quarter of a mile—which usually took a few minutes—in what seemed to her literally like no time. One second she was near the car and the next second she was home. She flew. She said her body seemed more suspended from the sky than lifting off the ground. At home, when she could breathe again, she was amazed at her own speed. Had she run as fast as she felt she had? She decided to time herself. The next day, she put on the same clothes, the same shoes, and walked to the alley. She imagined there was a car parked in the same spot and she tried to relive her fear and to remember how her body, legs, and feet felt when she ran home the night before. It took her exactly one minute, three seconds to run home. The next day she went to see the athletic director of her middle school, who timed her running and took her to the athletic director of the high school, who took her to the track coach of York University. The rest, as they say, is history."

"So the flasher episode turned out to be fortuitous," I say. "Man proposes, God disposes, or something like that."

"I would call it a mixed blessing. It got her on the Olympic track team. And it made her scared shitless of all men."

Rock stopped talking and motioned to Tony for another. My wine bottle, which had been recorked from the day before, was now empty. We sat in silence until Rock's drink came.

"So?" I prompt.

"I hate to tell you this," Rock says. "It seems like a betrayal of confidence."

I knew I would have to ask direct questions to get her to go on. But it wasn't simple curiosity, I assuaged my conscience, it was for a greater purpose—The Book. "Did she have boyfriends? Somehow I inferred from what you told me that she wasn't a 'natural' lesbian."

"I don't know if she was a lesbian at all," Rock says, "in spite of our love affair. And yes, she had boyfriends, but not for long. When the relationship heated up, she ran away ... right on the spot. She stayed in a relationship as long as the man kept his pants on. When the under shorts came off, she ran. Several boyfriends were left stupefied by her sudden departure from their apartment, hotel room, motel."

Rock's voice was dead serious, but I could barely hold back a burst of laughter. I could see the men, inflamed to bursting, their stiff penises pointed threateningly at Tina, and her Olympic dash out the door. I controlled myself the way I did in high school or at a funeral when a laughing fit was about to erupt, with shallow rapid breathing, like a woman in labor.

"She was a virgin when I met her," Rock said. "Nothing about *my* body scared her."

CHAPTER TWENTY-FOUR

Author Brings Publisher
Up to Date

"Amazing," Harry says about the Rock/Tina story. Then he gets up from behind his desk, comes over to me and pinches my cheek. "This book might be a winner," he says. "You're looking good, *madeleh.*"

I didn't know if he meant good to look at or good as a writer.

"How about some lunch," he says.

I'm always surprised when I leave Harry's office to find that it is daylight outside. I've never been there after dark, but somehow, when I leave, it always feels like I've been to a matinee and come out to unexpected daylight. Not that it's ever fully daylight in downtown Toronto. There's not enough space between the tops of buildings for the sun to shine for more than fifteen minutes in any one span, as it hikes from building to building. And by the time it reaches us on the ground it is muddied with shadows and smog. Harry takes my arm and leads me to where I knew he would lead me— Bubbaleh's Delicatessen. Everyone knows him there, and through him, me.

I knew he would order a Reuben. He asks me, "Your usual Caesar?" "No," I say, "a half corned beef on rye," pleased with myself for not being as predictable as he is, yet feeling guilty as an aspiring vegetarian who too often falls off the wagon. I am enmeshed in guilt these days, having to lie continuously to people who answer my fake 'love searches.' It helps that most of the responses come to the author's box. More people it seems want to talk about their experiences than to look for more. Not like Addict.

A bucket of brine holding dill pickles and dilled green tomatoes is already on the table, and we help ourselves until the sandwiches come. At a deli you can't be too fastidious about fingers dipped into the same pickle bucket, and at lunchtime in a downtown deli you have to be willing to talk several decibels above your usual level. Talking loud and fast I give Harry a synopsis of Alice and Georgie. And I mention Addict.

"George is so eager to talk to this Alice again, if she weren't middle aged and a woman, I would suspect he was interested in her. She seems to have fascinated him. And I ... I also interviewed an unusual man. Says he belongs to a support group of Personals addicts."

"Really!" Harry says. "Tell me more."

"Well, he's handsome and interesting, and apparently has the sexual appeal and charm of Casanova."

Harry stops chewing and looks at me intently.

"What?" I say to Harry. "Why are you looking at me that way?"

He hurriedly looks away, but I've seen something hurt and worried in his eyes that I don't understand.

It's raining when Harry and I leave the deli, falling in large silver dollops. Unlike the sunlight, they're unimpeded by tall buildings. People are cramped into doorways and under canopies, except for the few who walk along unhurriedly. The world is divided into two types of people, I think, those who run for cover when it rains and those who don't mind getting wet. I'm glad that I and my publisher are of the latter type. On the other hand, in all fairness, if I were dressed to the nines for, say, a book award luncheon, I would run, too.

At the corner, where Harry ascends to his office and I descend to the northbound subway, he says, "So, and you're going to see this addict again?"

"I told you, I am going to try to find a way to visit his support group, so I have to see him again."

"You don't really *have* to," Harry says, and goes on to invite me to his father's for Shabbat dinner.

"He's been complaining that he doesn't see you enough, and blames me for it."

It's a toss-up, who I'd rather be with, Harry or Jake Sympler, his adorable father. "Sure," I say. "I'll bring him flowers."

"Make it a plant," Harry says. "He doesn't like to see flowers die."

I think about Addict all the way home, and I wonder if he had ever been caught. Probably not, since he was still worried about getting caught. Had he ever fallen in love and found it painful to break off?

That evening I write the two letters I planned to send to his box number, one as myself, asking him to reconsider allowing me to visit the support group, and if not, at least agreeing to one more interview, seeing that he had rushed off so unceremoniously after the last one. The second letter was in the guise of a new responder, who says she has many exciting experiences to share. If he answered the second and not the first, I would have to utilize still another decoy—my gorgeous redheaded friend, Carolyn. This could get as farcical as an eighteenth-century comedy—one guy entering the room, one in the closet and another one under the bed.

CHAPTER TWENTY-FIVE

Alice Explains

"I'm sure I revealed a very ugly side of myself the last time we met," Alice says to Georgie, "a selfish bitch who leaves her loving husband because he is depressed and impotent, just when he needs her most. Loving husband? I don't know. I have forgotten how to judge love. He said he loved me but they all say that, don't they? And his word wasn't sterling. As to the depression, he didn't fall into depression like someone accidentally falls into a ditch. Before the depression he was warm and generous and interesting and fun. But he was also a liar and a trickster and a bull shitter. Not blarney-type bullshit. His was guru-and-savior-type bullshit. When he met someone in need of rescue, it was his hand—words, I mean—that threw the rope to the person dangling over a precipice. And he had an uncanny ability to recognize those danglers. That's how he got his jobs. Failing companies paid him from the bottom of their barrels to set them back on solid ground. He never could. So the job lasted until the company went under—a year, or two. Sometimes, when he could charm the company's creditors and suppliers, the dregs kept them going for a few years. I don't think I am helping myself in your eyes. I still sound like a bitch, don't I."

"Go on."

"Well, long before I cheated, he cheated. He went off for a weekend with a high school sweetheart who had come to town and looked him up. Very good looking. I saw her picture. I found out about the tryst by going through his suitcase the night before a 'business trip.' Bottle of champagne and reservations for a posh hotel in Buffalo."

Seeing the expression of distaste on Georgie's face, Alice adds, "He was supposed to be going to   to sell an insurance policy to the

76

owner of a garbage collection company. I examined his suitcase because he had been acting very suspiciously."

"That was decent of him," Georgie says, "acting suspiciously. Shows he had a conscience."

"That's one way to look at it." Alice says. "Not my way. I think for many years he had been borrowing money from unsavory people, maybe Mafia loan sharks. He pressured me to sign for a second mortgage on our home, and I did, without ever knowing what the money was for, exactly. He said something about investing in the company he was working for at the time. So, conscience? George, I'm not going to continue the laundry list of my husband's faults. I just wanted to show you I wasn't as callous as you might have thought. I think his depression was brought on by guilt. It works that way, I think. Sometimes. Thanks for meeting me," she says, and begins to rise from her seat.

"Wait," Georgie says, and places his hand on hers. "You haven't told me how you got over your phobias."

"Call me," she says.

CHAPTER TWENTY-SIX

I Show Gladwell What I Have
Written So Far

A WEEK AFTER I READ GA's brisk discrediting of my reasons for writing this book, I bring him a draft of the chapters I'd written. "I just want you to know," I say, annoyed with the apologetic tone of my voice, "I want you to know that this is not the final version. I know it needs rewriting."

"As I've often said to my students, nothing is written until it is rewritten. Well, sit down if you want to stay while I read it. If not, absent yourself and I'll be in touch."

I probably make a mistake by staying but I want to observe his facial expressions and body language as he reads.

I don't have to wait long to see that familiar skeptical, slight inclination of his head and the lift of his right eyebrow. He sighs. There are all kinds of sighs, just as there are all kinds of laughs— chuckles, guffaws, chortles, snickers, peels, giggles, titters. This is a sigh of exasperation.

He says in his most academician voice, "You know as well as I that every book needs a situation of tension. Someone or something must press against an obstacle, someone or something prevents what should happen from happening. There must be a hurdle, a fence, a wall, an enemy, which the protagonist must leap, scale, or tear down. In the case of investigative non fiction the writer is the protagonist."

"A wall?" I say. "That reminds me of a joke (which I tell in order to have time to formulate an answer precise and succinct enough to satisfy him). "There was an old, old man who went to pray at the Western Wall in Jerusalem every single day for over seventy years. A reporter gets wind of it and thinks it would make a good human-interest story. The reporter investigates. Is it true you haven't missed a day in 70 years? True, the old man answers. What do you pray for every day? I pray for peace in the world. I pray for the end of starvation. I pray the rich should share with the poor. But none of that has happened, the reporter points out. How does that make you feel? I feel, says the old man, like I'm talking to a wall."

"Funny," Gladwell says, but he makes no sound that resembles laughter.

"I already told you what the 'wall' is," I say. "It is our culture. Our culture insists that marriage is good, marriage is the goal of our maturity, marriage keeps society from falling into chaos, into nihilism. Yet our modern life makes marriage difficult to attain and even more difficult to sustain."

"Quite," he says, and gives me a long indecipherable look, somewhere between admiration and pity.

"Quite what?" I say.

"Quite interesting," he says. "Quite amusing." And he goes on reading.

At he end he says, "Quite absorbing, but I still see no evidence that you really understand why you are writing this."

"I'll say it again," I say, my voice rising to a crescendo that suggests a tightly controlled scream, "Western society has become unglued. Personals are one way people are trying to restick it."

He ignores me and goes on, "The stories of individuals build the structure of your book. But in order to get at the real meaning of your book, we have to de-construct it. After you remove each individual story; after you remove the, shall we say, significance of each story and the compound significance of all the stories added together, what remains?"

"Nothing remains." I say.

"What remains is the reason you are writing this book. What remains is what your book is about."

"You are talking nonsense." I dare mutter, but his pontification isn't exhausted.

"Literary critics take a book apart as though they were dissecting a frog to see how the book functions. When you put the parts back together you have a frog. But *deconstructing* doesn't examine the parts; or rather, it examines the parts to see what is *not* there. Only by seeing what is *not* there can you grasp what *is* there. Biologists are not concerned with what is not there when they dissect a frog. But if a literary deconstructionist were to dissect a frog, he would see that what is not there is a horse, a man, a star. What is not there is the marsh water the frog comes from. What is not there is the scientist who is doing the dissecting. And perhaps most telling in the entire process is to understand *why* the biologist feels it is important to dissect the frog in the first place. All of these discoveries must be part of any conclusion regarding the meaning of the frog. "You are a pretty smart cookie," GA says, dipping into an archaic vernacular. "As I deconstruct your book, I find the marsh water and the frog's food supply. Do I find the biologist? Not yet."

CHAPTER TWENTY-SEVEN

Mr. Crenshaw from the Support Group

SOMETIMES ONE CAN INTERCEPT one's own stupidity. My plan to write to Addict's box in the guise of a new respondent was a frightening brain lapse. I forgot to ask myself *then what?* Why would he throw open the gates of the support group to my friend Carolyn any more readily than to me?

I did send the honest letter, requesting a second interview. I shouldn't have been so surprised that he agreed. I was, after all, a new support group of one, with whom he could showcase his shenanigans in complete confidence.

When I arrive at the hotel bar where I had first met him, however, I'm approached by a man I'd never seen.

"You must be Sylvia," he says. "Boyd's description was good."

He hands me a note: "This is Mr. Crenshaw from the support group. Since the support group is your primary interest in meeting me again, I thought a second view would be more helpful to you than I would."

I am unnerved, disappointed, and flustered.

"I hope you don't mind the substitution," Mr. Crenshaw says.

I mind the substitution enormously, but I locate my dignity and reply, "Not at all. I am so grateful to you for agreeing to this."

Presumably, Boyd has explained my purpose, so when we are seated at one of the minute tables, I start right in, "Mr. Crenshaw, I need to know from as many people as possible why they advertise. Why did you sit yourself down and type yourself into an inch or so of space, not impulsively, in a moment of anger or despair, which you then crumple into the wastebasket or shred into the toilet or burn over the stove; but with continued intention you put it into an envelope and mail it the next day, having had eight hours to sleep on it? Why?"

Mr. Crenshaw had been leaning toward me. Now he leans against the back of his chair and beckons to the waiter, orders a Rob Roy and inclines his head toward me. "A very dry Reisling," I say.

"Are you married?" I ask.

"Yes," he says, "and you can call me Kurt."

"I hope you won't be."

One side of his mouth lifts at my feeble joke. Still upset that Boyd sent this understudy instead of himself, I go on as aggressively as before: "Why did you leave your wife lying in the bed alone with her navel, her breasts, her vagina, etc., etc. and steal into your den in the middle of the night to hammer out those thirty or fifty words?"

"The way you state your question," he responds, "carries a very negative judgment of me."

"No," I disclaim. "Only trying to understand."

"Oh, no," he calls my bluff. "Alone with her navel, etc. is a judgment. But I will explain. I did it because I could not not." And Kurt goes on with an explanation that sounds so much like Boyd's that I wonder if they had conspired to put me on.

"Some things you do because you must do them, and some things you do because you cannot not do them. The former category includes dental examinations and going to work. But I am being disingenuous. I know what you want to know: Why did I go into my den, removing my body from within inches of a perfectly adequate woman, with all her parts intact. Indeed, a woman more attractive than most. But a woman, you see. One. Only one. So that with her I too was only one. Just me. A single, limited man, eight years older than I was when I married her. I have a need to be more than one man, to multiply myself. I need to be seen the way a housefly sees, in myriad lenses—a dozen of me, a hundred of me. I've found those eyes through Personals. A wife doesn't see as a fly sees. A wife sees as a telescope sees—me far away and diminished, or as a microscope sees—me with every blemish enlarged—idealized or despised, but only one."

My God, I thought. Is this a male disease, this inability to be satisfied with just one woman? I recalled visiting the San Diego

Zoo a few years ago, going around in one of those little trams with a zoo tour guide. We passed a pair of some sort of deer in a large open pen, each one grazing by itself, completely ignoring the other. A male and a female, the guide told us. They may have recently mated, so the male is not at all interested in her, "But put a new female in there with him and he'll be on top of her in a minute."

As a woman I was appalled. Also worried. But as a writer, I understood Kurt's and Boyd's feelings. To them women were what my writing was to me. I carried a head full of unexpressed thoughts and a heart full of longing for the perfect but anonymous audience. I speak to no one so well as to my writing. I am a different person with every piece I write, with every character.

"And do you accomplish that?" I ask. "Do you become more?"

He laughs. "Therein lies a tale."

"Are you going to tell me the tale?"

"Sure. Why not? That's why I'm here, isn't it?" He looks at his watch. "I have a half hour. I'll make it short."

"The unexpected and unwanted happened. I fell madly in love with one of the Persons, and she with me. I stopped placing ads. I no longer even glanced at another woman. I no longer wanted to be many men, just her one man. I divorced my wife and married her.

"But my love kept a secret she didn't divulge until several months after I married her, when honesty was forced upon her: We met an old friend of hers on the street. The friend said, 'Well, hello Julie! Hello Bill!' My name, of course, is not Bill. When I pressed her for an explanation, she told me that I was the spitting image of a man who left her. She showed me his picture. I am his duplicate. You probably can't imagine how unnerving and diminishing it is to be someone's clone. Not only wasn't I more men than one, I was half a man. The other half was another man.

"Well, I divorced her, too, and I was again a man with multiple selves."

"So, you're not married now?"

I am. I fell in love again. Met her through Personals. Married again. Vowed to stay married this time. But continued with Personals."

"Why?"

"Same reason. Same reason as before. But therein lies another tale."

"*You* could write a book," I say "My Life as a Personals User. Will you tell me about the second 'therein'?"

"I'll think about it. Probably not. I wouldn't want it in the book. It was different. Important."

I leave the meeting with Kurt, feeling very much in the need of Harry's company, or even Gladwell's or Georgie's.

Georgie rings me up. Says he's coming over. Bringing dinner.

CHAPTER TWENTY-EIGHT

Gladwell Fills in Author's
Back Story

I TRUST, DEAR READER, that you would like to know a bit more about Sylvia. For you she materialized out of thin air on the first page of this book. You know little beyond what she herself chooses to reveal to you. But as with us all, certain events of her past elucidate her present.

I have known her since she enrolled in my graduate course "Women in Literature." I later supervised her Master's thesis on Jane Austen, "More Sensibility than Sense," a remarkable study which I urged her to have published, but she was off to other pursuits, men not being one of them. They came with the territory. The territory Ted came with was Earth Day.

It was organized by three members of the faculty: one from biology, one from sociology, and me, from English. No one from Environmental Studies, since that department was heavily endowed by the Monsanto Corporation. We three professors gathered a group of our most devoted students to form an Earth Day Committee. Sylvia's job was to outfit a bus with ecological displays and drive it around campus, using a bullhorn to attract students: "Come see what's in here!" she blared. "Your life depends on it! Come on in! It's free!" The bus contained a lung in a bottle, blackened and porous from the addiction of its former owner to the tobacco industry; three jars of deformed embryos, showing the effects of mercury poisoning at various stages of development; a short film on population explosion, which supported Malthus's prognostications that earth could not sustain its projected billions; charts that showed the disappearance of vast rain forests under the blades of lumber companies, and dollhouse-sized models of products made from rainforest wood.

Ted was in charge of distributing hundreds of Cedar and Spruce seedlings to children who were bussed to campus for an Earth Day field trip, along with instructions on how to plant them back home in their yards.

At the end of the day there was a party for volunteers. Ted arrived wearing a seedling in his baseball cap and carrying a bouquet of seedlings tied with a green ribbon for the girl who ran the "Catastrophe Bus."

They had much in common—concern about the eco system and anger at social injustice—child labor, abuse of women, and the gigantic salaries of corporate CEOs.

When Ted agreed to read a poem at a World Trade Organization protest march, our author knew he was the man for her. When they graduated, he suggested they move to Newmarket and 'set up shop' together. She would find some sort of writing job—journalism, small regional newspaper to start, and he would strike out on his own as a real estate lawyer. By then she had been in love with him for two years, and though he never pronounced the words "I love you," she was sure he did.

After a while, his failure to say the word 'love' became a sort of running joke: She would chide, "When are you going to say I love you?" And he would say, "When you become rich," or "when you become famous." And they would laugh. Or she would say, "How come you love me so much?" And he would grin. Or she would say, "Love, love, love, you're always talking about love." And he would smile.

Seven years. Many friends, nice apartment, sufficient money, and they continued to look at the world around them in the same way. They were, shall we say, compatible. Seven years of daily okayness interspersed with high highs and low lows, in other words, a normal relationship.

"Who is Sylvia, what is she, that all the swains commend her," are the Shakespearean lines that inspired her parents. Ted was not a swain.

When he left her, he uttered the word "Personals." Perhaps that word lingered in her subconscious mind and years later outed as the muse of this book.

CHAPTER TWENTY-NINE

Backstory: Sylvia and Ted Part Ways

"I'M TOO GOOD FOR YOU!" Sylvia's voice rose to a pitch that signaled many screeching conclusions to come.

"You are right." Ted said.

"You're right, you're right," Sylvia mocked loudly. "You think by admitting that I am right, that makes you superior, that makes *you* right. I don't care how many times you admit it. You can admit that I am too good for you a thousand times, and that doesn't change the fact that I *am* too good for you!"

There was no way to resolve this. Nothing for him to do but remain calm, look out the window at the cloudless morning sky and unruffled leaves, fiddle with some books in the bookcase and wait.

Sylvia's hysteria, as Ted thought of it, drew Susan, her former college roommate who happened to be visiting them, from the next room. She stood in the doorway for a moment, watching Sylvia hunched on the sofa on the verge of tears, and Ted rearranging books.

"She's right, you know."

Ted's anger began to rise. Two against one. Now he had to respond.

"She knows damned well I care for her. I am always concerned for her welfare."

"You're a stone, Ted," Sylvia sobbed from the sofa. "You're a stone. A stone."

"Yeah, you probably do care," Susan interjected again, "but you *are* a stone. Look at your face. Sylvia's bawling and your face is like the cover of the book you're holding."

Sylvia cried louder at this empathetic remark and now Susan was fully involved. "Do you remember when you were a kid and someone would come up to you and say, 'Close your eyes and stick out your hands.' And you would be torn between suspicion and anticipation, 'What do you have?' And they'd insist, 'Uh, uh.' And sometimes you'd get a gumball or a marble. But sometimes you'd get some torn grass or a thumbtack or dirt from the curb. That's what you did, Ted. You asked her to close her eyes and stick out her hands, and you put dirt in them."

Ted wondered what Susan was remembering to come up with that analogy, to which there was no possible response. What 'dirt' did she have in mind? He could only squirm.

He got his overcoat while she was talking, as unperturbed as though he were alone in the room. Before leaving, he stopped beside Sylvia and put his hand on her shoulder. "I'll call you later." She shrugged off his hand.

His mood lightened when he slammed the car door and continued to grow sunnier as he drove to work. The day was fine, pollution low, the tops of high-rise buildings were outlined sharply inside a bright blue sky.

The good-looking girl who worked at the magazine stand in the lobby of the office tower perked up and widened her eyes in welcome as he approached, as he did every weekday for coffee and the morning paper. The few friendly words they exchanged added up to a brief history: She was a freelance photographer just getting established in her career. She was attractive to him, and, he hoped, attracted by him. She had fine, sandy brown silky hair that hung almost to her slim waist. He couldn't get a look at her legs behind the counter, but he imagined them long and slim and shapely. He hated bulging calves, and didn't want her to have them. Her eyes were unusually light, a transparent gray, almost silver.

But he had made a non-adultery pact with Sylvia when they moved in together—free will, not legal, and all the more significant, it seemed to him.

But ... as the story goes ... one day ...

And this was that day.

When he approached the stand, she was about to run to the mailbox to mail an answer to a Personals ad, she tells him. She wonders if he could please watch the stand for just a second? The mailbox is right over there.

As she runs he sees that her legs are long and slim and shapely, no bulging calves, and as she runs her long, light brown hair lifts in the breeze.

When she returns he says. "Maybe you won't need an answer to your letter. Maybe I am the one you're looking for."

Two weeks later, he and Sylvia parted ways.

CHAPTER THIRTY

Georgie Reports: Alice
Interviewing Over

A COUPLE OF HOURS after I got home from my interview with Kurt Crenshaw, Georgie arrived wearing workout clothes and bearing a quart of chickpea and spinach soup and a whole-grain baguette. While I warmed the soup he put on a vinyl of Ella. We ate in silence, as if it was a sin to talk over "The Marvelous One."

"So ... You're not seeing Alice again?"

"No. Not again. You have enough for the book."

"I'm glad. I wasn't comfortable with the direction your 'interviews' with the platinum-haired Alice seemed to be going."

"Nothing to worry about," he says with an edge of annoyance unusual for Georgie and looking into the distance. "I'm meeting Randy at the club. See you on Thursday."

Two days later, Georgie brings more information for the book and then says, "I have an appointment with Alice tomorrow. She called. Asked if I didn't want to know how she got over her phobias."

"And of course you did."

Georgie ignores my sarcastic tone. "I *had* been wondering. Did she see a shrink? Or during all those years since her divorce did she lay awake nights listening for a stair to creak or a screen to slide open? Who did she scream for when she saw a spider? How long did the golf pro last?"

"Okay," I say. "Okay, okay. Let me know."

CHAPTER THIRTY-ONE

Appointments and Disappointments

Rock phoned to find out when the book would be published. She's counting on it to resurrect Tina. Disappointments should not be conveyed by telephone so I made a date to see her at the bar that very evening.

Beautiful Blythe phoned to invite me to a party at her home—a benefit for the Toronto String Quartet. I was too surprised to do anything but stall. I would call her back.

I broke down and phoned Boyd to thank him for setting up the interview with his support group colleague, Kurt Crenshaw. "I still wish you would allow me to continue my interview with you," I said.

"Can we talk at dinner?" he asked. His voice was as thrilling on the phone as it had been during our interview.

I was instantly unnerved and tongue-tied. Was he inviting himself to dinner at my place or inviting me out? Was this an interview or a date? Confusing invitation. After a too long silence, I could think of nothing to say except, "I'm only a middling cook."

He laughed. "I had in mind the Shangri La. Are you free Saturday night?"

I skipped all the quips surrounding the word "free," and said, "Yes. I'd love to," for which I was immediately sorry, since it was a response for a date invitation, not an interview. Actually, Harry and I were supposed to go to a poetry reading at the U of T bookstore Saturday night, but that would be easy to break. The more troublesome conflict was an early Saturday evening interview with a man who had answered "Middle-Aged Married Woman."

CHAPTER THIRTY-TWO

Back at Tony's Bar and Grill

TONY'S IS SO CROWDED I can hardly find Rock, whose five-foot-two is immersed in the crowd. She is wearing, a shirt, a vest, a cap, and jodhpurs. She often wears these, I learn, as an alternative to jeans.

"Hey, Sylvie," she says. She had lopped off the last syllable of my name as my friends did, within five minutes of our first meeting. "How about my apartment? It's too loud in here and everyone is bugging me about when I'll deliver my new story."

Her apartment is ... well, quaint. It is one large triangular room. One angle holds a sofa, chairs, and floor pillows. Another angle holds the necessaries for cooking and dining. And one angle is occupied by a drafting table that serves as a desk and is strewn with soft and hard porn magazines whose pictures she says she describes when she can't come up with a visual image of her own. A staircase spirals up from the center of the triangle into her loft bedroom. Green-tinted windows circle the entire top of the isosceles length of the triangle, and admit plenty of light, but not an inch of view from anywhere but the bedroom portholes. The floors are wooden, very worn and highly waxed, giving them the appearance of old barn-wood glazed with glass. The walls are bare cement block, with each of the three areas painted a different color. Low bookshelves constructed of brick uprights and wooden planks lean against the walls and are filled with books, plants, and odd gewgaws. The ceiling is painted navy blue and over the entire surface glow luminescent stars, such as one might find in a child's bedroom.

"Make yourself at home. Beer, wine, or booze?"

"Whatever you're having."

I settle myself comfortably on the deep-cushioned slipcovered sofa, itching to make a round of the bookshelves, but not wanting to seem nosey. I hear the clink of ice cubes and then Rock bearing two manhattans without maraschino cherries. She sits across from me in a large lounge chair. Her feet in their riding boots stick out in front of her like a child's. Her five-feet-two spans the kind of body I had always thought of as 'peasant'—solid and large boned, with heavy breasts and strong calves. Compact for a woman of fifty, or maybe fifty-five. Maybe sixty. Hard to tell.

"Great place," I say. "How in the world did you get the stars up there? Must have needed scaffolding. They're wonderful." I wondered why she didn't have pictures on the walls, and I'm clumsy at diplomatic shrouding of plain language, but I try, "And your walls are so tastefully minimalist."

She doesn't let me get away with my stab at tact. "You're wondering why I don't have any pictures. I don't have any, because I want hundreds of them, not just three or four hung up forever. And even if I published *Hustler* I wouldn't earn enough to buy the ones I really like. So I hang my pictures in museums and go look at them there."

After a couple of gulps of her manhattan that almost empty the glass, she launches into a barrage of questions that would have annoyed me if I hadn't liked her from the moment I met her—the second moment, that is—when she reconsidered her anger and came back in through the door she had stormed out of.

"You're not married," she states inclining her head toward my unadorned left hand.

"Right."

"Ever been?"

"No."

"Boyfriend?"

"No. Once upon a time."

"No happily ever after."

"Happily, but not with him."

"With who?"

"Just me."

"So you're a happy solitaire?"

"Well. Yes."

"I'm not," she says, "Not at all."

With that she finishes her drink and goes for a refill. She sees I'm not ready for another and doesn't ask just to be polite.

The interruption gives me an opportunity to terminate the subject of me and open the one I wanted to know more about.

"You haven't told me why Tina left."

Her usual cheerful bluster changes to quiet dejection. "I wish I knew. I thought we were a happy pair."

I would dare to say what I am about to say to very few people. I hardly know Rock, but her openness invites openness. "Rock," I say, "I don't see how one person in a relationship could be very happy and not know the other one is very unhappy. Didn't you talk to each other about your feelings, or intuit each other's feelings?" The minute I said this I was sorry I didn't use the third person instead of second person.

Rock's mouth droops and I'm afraid she is going to cry. "If you're right, then we weren't happy. I was happy, and I dumped my happiness onto her unsuspecting body. She must have been miserable, enduring me." I move to the arm of her chair and try to comfort her.

"Rock, we will find her and you will learn the truth. I promise." And now I have to inform her about the realities of small press publishing—the long wait to get into print, the miniscule readership compared with the millions who read newspapers. "Let's do this," I inject into her disappointment. "Let's put ads in the Personals pages of every newspaper we can think of. Either Tina or someone who knows her is sure to see one of them."

"From your lips to God's ears," she says.

"Do you believe in God, Rock?"

"Neh. Just a habit. I don't believe in anything. You have to know *something* for sure to believe in God, and the only thing I know for sure is that we're all going to die. Every last one of us, good and bad, saint and sinner. Knowing that makes everyone as precious as if there was a god and he made them. I look at someone and when I remember to remember that they are going to die, not maybe, but for sure—they have this one little life and they're so serious about it—it makes me want to hug them and stroke their hair and grab them around the waist and dance with them. Dance them around and around until we can't do anything but fall in a heap laughing."

She brightens with hope and before I leave we compose an ad to run in the *Sun, Globe, Star, National Post,* and in all the dozens of small regional free papers in the GTA.

Composing the ad wasn't easy. Formal and businesslike might not evoke an answer. Pathos and love might scare Tina away from further contact. Should the ad dishonestly invent an urgent need, like Rock on her deathbed? Or invent a bait like a newly discovered inheritance? We decide to keep it simple, honest, and moderately emotional:

Dearest Tina, my friend, please get in touch with me. No pressure, no expectations. I respect your freedom. I just want to know how you are. Rock." In the same ad, we write, "I am looking for Tina the track coach. If you know where to find her, please deliver my message. Or call me at (416) — ——, collect if you are out of the GTA."

CHAPTER THIRTY-THREE

Georgie's Interview with
a Straight Jewish Man

I CAN'T KEEP UP with the letters and phone calls, the number of appointments I have to make. I simply have to ignore many replies to my ads. Sometimes with hardly a hurried glance. It is terrible to think that lost loves have come over the transom and are lying in a slush pile. I'm sure that some fascinating Persons lie undiscovered or discarded. Every one I have interviewed is fascinating in one way or another, and when Georgie or I can get them talking, they all have a story to tell, some twist on the theme of mate search. My rationalization for winnowing the plethora—in my mind I see a yearning man or woman sitting by the phone or daily dashing to the mailbox—is that even people who place legitimate Personals aren't obligated to respond to every letter. But I do try, and now I have double booked for Saturday night, both with men. Luckily, Georgie, who is usually out stomping the yard on Saturday night, is available with his tape recorder.

Poor Georgie. He has to be very kind, very patient, very sensitive, and very inventive to calm all the people who respond to my deceptive ads. This time he has to deal with a man who had answered the ad from "Married Woman." I'm worried that he may encounter instant ire that could spill over into murderous rage, as in the movie *Brokeback Mountain.* Or have to fend off a repressed sexual proclivity that had been smoldering under wife and kids. I don't know what Georgie can expect. But I do know that he has the gift of calming volatile situations.

My anxiety was well founded. He tells me about the meeting and runs the tape of the interview the next morning at my place, over coffee. "You're not going to find anything like this in the Sunday *Times,*" he says.

"Please," Georgie hurries to say to the man who conforms to the description in the letter. "This isn't a pickup. Please let me explain. The woman who called you is a writer. She did lie to get you here, but it wasn't a homosexual lie. It was a journalistic lie."

The man's jawbone and hands relax a little, allowing Georgie to explain the whole project, which he does in such poetic terms that by the second Bombay Sapphire martini (Georgie can be very generous with my expense account), they are not only conversing like friends, but Irvin is permitting George to turn on the tape recorder, and is admitting that he also lied. In his response to the ad, he had stated that he was never married, but in fact he was and is, which is the reason he was looking for a married woman— discreet and less demanding, holidays already occupied, second finger left hand already appropriated.

"It's the Jewish mother syndrome," he tells Georgie, naming a syndrome Georgie had never heard of. "Jewish and mother and marriage are an indivisible troika; they're all on one harness. I couldn't have a non-Jewish mother for my kids. In my mind she wouldn't be a mother. And actually the kids wouldn't be Jewish. Are you Jewish?" He continues after Georgie shakes his head, "That's according to Jewish matrilineal law—Jewishness is passed down by the woman. So when I married Robin, a *shikseh*, she had to convert.

"So what's the problem? My kids have a Jewish mother and I have a wife. But I don't. I have two Jewish mothers. That blonde *shiksehhood* is what turned me on. Jewish women don't excite me. Jewish women are all stand-ins for my mother. When Robin was my girlfriend she had long legs, small breasts, and honey-colored silky hair. But now that she converted to Jew and became my wife, her physical appearance is just a disguise. I can't remember having one incestuous feeling as a boy. I didn't like my mother to touch me, and not because of any unconscious taboo. If Freud had analyzed me, his whole Oedipal *schtick* would be different.

"Hey, don't get the wrong idea. Don't think I'm a repressed homosexual, that I really wanted my father. But I'll tell you, even if I was queer, I wouldn't be queer for Jewish men. They'd be too much like my mother.

97

"So, I'm a good husband and son at home and I play around outside, and Personals are the easiest and safest game. I own a manufacturing company. I have more money than I know what to do with, and I'm not one of those CEOs whose appetite for money keeps getting bigger. See my stomach? Flat, right? That shows you I'm not greedy. My company keeps getting bigger and my wealth keeps growing all by itself. That's the secret rich people don't divulge. Once you have a certain amount of money, a critical mass, it expands all by itself. Thank God my belly isn't like that."

"How do you get that critical mass?" Georgie asks eagerly.

"How old are you?"

"Twenty-eight."

"About fifteen years too late. You have to want money when you're twelve, and you have to start making it. I don't mean mowing lawns and delivering paper. I mean smart things like selling candy bars to kids at school for twice the price you paid for them, because there's no stores around and those kids really want one, *now*. Like running a gift exchange business; no one gets what they want for Hanukah, so you arrange for an exchange—Joe gets Irving's baseball glove and Irving gets Joe's transformer and the middleman gets two bucks.

"Women are the only frontier left for me to conquer. I know that's a cliché, but each strange woman is a wilderness and I get to the Promised Land through some of them. Afterward, looking back over my shoulder, I see it was only a small oasis in Canaan, and the Promised Land is still ahead of me in the desert. But for a minute I get the feeling that I have arrived there.

"Do homosexuals feel that way? With all due respect, they're much more promiscuous than most heterosexuals? They must. Or is it pure lust?"

Georgie nods, smiles, looks non-committal. Irwin doesn't wait for an answer.

"I wander through deserts of work, home, wife, streets, restaurants, business meetings, bars, and sometimes I find a small oasis. If I were a poet my oasis might be words. I don't want to brag but I'm a poet of the prick. I write with my rod."

There was a click as the recorder tape ran out.

I hadn't so much as glanced at the *Times*. "Whoa," I say to Georgie. "He's an original. Too bad he didn't tell you about any actual Personals relationship. We need those for the book. Are you going to see him again?"

"We'll see," Georgie says. "He's supposed to phone me when he feels like talking. If he does, maybe I can get him to come out from behind all those *Exodus* metaphors."

CHAPTER THIRTY-FOUR

Shabbat Dinner with Jake Sympler

JAKE WAS STILL PREPARING dinner when I arrived before Harry at the Sympler home. It had been too long since I visited. Even at seventy, you could tell where Harry got his charm and his sweetness. We would be eating before sundown, one of the many liberties Jake took with traditional Judaism. I was sure the menu would be traditional, as always, though. After the candle lighting and prayers over the wine and bread, we would have chicken soup with either matzo balls or noodles, followed by some kind of roasted chicken, accompanied by some kind of vegetable, probably sweet and sour carrots, and some kind of starch—I hoped it would be the apple-raison kugel which Jake had perfected to the status of haute cuisine. He greeted me the same way Harry did, with a "hello *Medeleh*" and a kiss on the cheek.

I gave him a hug and handed him the small hibiscus, loaded with buds at every stage of opening.

"Will this die?" he asks.

"No it won't. When these flowers are gone, it will bloom again. In the summer you can put it out on your porch and take it inside before the first frost. Here's a card with 'Care of a hibiscus.'"

"You are precious. If I had a daughter ...." he says, as he always does when I visit, though usually Harry is around to receive his father's meaningful glance.

My offer to help in the kitchen is refused. I put on a recording of Billie Holiday and I'm about to leaf through the inside pages of today's newspaper or *Quill & Quire*, when I notice the photograph album lying next to it.

"Jake," I call to the kitchen. "Can I look at this?"

"I put it out just for you to look at," he calls back.

I don't flip at random. I start from page one: A hugely smiling couple, the man unmistakably a young Jake Sympler, hold between them an infant Harry. Then a photo of Harry in a playpen, crying. Harry in a baby swing, looking incredibly happy. Harry in a high chair, barely recognizable behind tomato sauce and noodles smeared from forehead to neck. When I get to Harry-the-toddler, about age three, I say "Oh, my!" loud enough to draw Jake from the kitchen. "He's gorgeous," I say, about the perfectly featured face, surrounded by a halo of golden curls.

"Isn't he?" Jake *keveled.*

"Isn't he what?" Harry asks, having let himself in and entered the living room.

"Gorgeous," Jake says. "Just like now."

"Oh for God's sake, dad. Have you pressed that album on Sylvia?"

"Not at all!" Jake protests. "It was on the table. Anyway, you're almost late. Dinner is ready. Sylvia, will you do us the honor of blessing the candles?"

"Only if I can have the album back after dinner."

Jake beams "Of course!" and Harry shakes his head in exasperation.

I do continue studying the album after dinner, while Harry and his father clear the table and do the dishes.

Of course, I knew the outlines of Harry's life. His mother died when he was seventeen. He went to college in the States—Brandeis University. After completing his sophomore year with grades so low he barely squeaked into junior level, he dropped out and joined the army. His father was horrified, terrified, and totally perplexed, but Harry had convinced himself that entering the Gulf War was a moral, patriotic, and humanist duty. I knew this, still, seeing Harry's mischievous grin, jaunty cap on head, corporal stripes on sleeve, in one shot performing a mock salute, startled me. I started to write a poem in my head: "Young soldier, crisp and clean. . ."

I turned more album pages—Harry shooting baskets. Harry up at bat. Harry dancing. Hmm. Who's the girl?

By now the two men had joined me in the living room.

"Haven't you had enough?" Harry asks. His voice is non-committal. Was he pleased or annoyed?

"I haven't seen any graduation pictures," I say. Where's the gown and mortarboard?"

Harry and Jake look at each other. "Didn't you know?" Jake says. "Harry didn't tell you? After the army, Harry never went back to the university. He didn't tell me. I kept giving him money for tuition and books. He came home only at the times he would have been home on vacation."

"Harry!" I expostulate. "I didn't know you were capable of such duplicity."

"I was then," he says. "We're talking about ages twenty to twenty-three. And my father would never have agreed to what I wanted to do."

Naturally, I ask what it was he wanted to do.

"He came out of the service wanting to write the Great Canadian War Story," Jake says.

I turn to look expectantly at Harry.

"I wrote it," he says. "For a year. Finished it. Sent it out all over the place. I had scruples about using the Sympler Books connection. Half the books that are published are editors' or publishers' quid pro quos. I wanted my book to be accepted cold, for itself alone. It wasn't."

"Where is it now?" I ask.

"In a country graveyard." he says, alluding to Goldsmith's famous poem.

But Jake was not going to allow his son to portray himself in such a deprecatory light. "You know what he did then? While I thought he was piling up thirty-five credit hours a semester at Brandies, he was sitting in the New York public library, reading eight to ten hours a day. When he came out, he worked with me at Sympler Books and when he was twenty-nine, I turned the company over to him and got out of the way. He's the one who made it one of the most prestigious small presses in Canada, on par with America's top three."

"Fathers." Harry says, shaking his head.

I smile, shelving the many thoughts I would have to ruminate over at length when I got home, and return to the album. Harry on a horse, next to another horse with a very pretty girl on it. Then more pages of Harry swimming with a girl, Harry dancing with a girl, Harry just standing, posing for the picture with a girl on his arm. I murmur, "Lots of girls," without looking up.

"Yeah," Jake says. "Harry always had lots of girls, but he has only been in love with one woman. He's a late bloomer."

"Dad, please!" Harry says, sounding genuinely angry.

CHAPTER THIRTY-FIVE

Tying Up Some Loose Ends

HARRY MUST BE WRITING. He answers the office phone before the second ring, and he doesn't sound impatient. I must be interrupting a blank page.

"Ho," he says.

"Ho?" I say. "Am I supposed to respond with 'Hey, dude?'"

"Hi, *Medeleh*," he instantly changes eras and ethnicities, "How are you?"

"I have to break our Saturday night date."

"Why? What's up?"

Should I refer to it as a date, an appointment, or an interview?

"I'm meeting Boyd Adams."

"The Addict? Haven't you talked to him twice, already?"

"No," I say, "Just once."

"Well, no date breaking on the phone," he says. "Analogy: Love letters are wonderful, but Dear John letters are mean things. You'll have to do it in person," he says and hangs up.

What's the matter with Harry, I wonder. Must be having a very trying day. I'd stop in and see him.

When I return Blythe's call, she repeats her invitation to the fundraiser at her home. I'm sure the acceptable donation would not be a hundred or two. It would be thousands, scores of thousands, more scores maybe than a benefit dinner at a rented venue, no matter how exclusive. A benefit at Blythe and Barry's home was serious business; it meant the hosts' hearts were in it. I was honest in my refusal—no previous engagement, no houseguest, no out-of-town: I say that I can't afford what would be considered a minimally respectable donation, had nothing in my closet appropriate to wear, and couldn't afford to buy an outfit. I hated myself for my clincher—

"I'm just a poor writer."

She was honest, too. She doesn't say that I'm rich in talent or that I'd be beautiful no matter what I wore. She says, "I knew that before I called you. We will contribute in your name—an amount beyond what we would ordinarily give. So it wouldn't be there, if you weren't. And you could choose anything from my closet to wear. You could come over that afternoon and my hairdresser and makeup person could do us both. Please, Sylvia. I would really love to have you there. Talking to you would save me from an evening of unrelieved hostessing."

"Wear your clothes?"

"Please. I have dresses I've never worn in this city. And I'm sure you're about my size. It isn't a ball gown and tuxedo kind of affair. Just a party. Please?"

"Won't everyone be half a couple?"

"Not everyone, but if you have someone who could escort you, that would be just fine."

"I'm thinking of my publisher. If he says yes, I'll say yes."

"Do you want me to call him?"

"No. I'll ask him."

Even though I would be stopping at his office the next day, because of his insistence on face-to-face date breaking, I call Harry right back. His page must still be blank. He picks up on half a ring. He agrees without hesitation, apparently less intimidated by the whole idea than I am.

"I only have a minute," I say the minute I enter his office the next day. "And this is my formal, official, in person Saturday night date cancellation." Then I tell him about my last meeting with Rock, the newspaper ads I placed for her, and my admission to her that the book would be a very unreliable mode for locating a missing person.

"But you're still putting the story in the book? Everything about Tina—her screwball phobia and lesbian interlude? If you identify Rock, you'll be identifying her, you know. Won't you be revealing too much?"

"If I reveal less, there's no story."

But Harry has touched a nerve that renews my doubts about

the book. I say to him what I've said to Gladwell: "Sometimes I feel that Personals and all our other ways of finding a mate are silly and fruitless. Is our own choice better than accepting what the universe throws in our path, arranged by parents or community or the happenstance of just being the only available one around? Whether they're short or fat or ignorant or gentle or intelligent or kind or stingy or brutal, etc, etc. etc., are they any worse than what our own choice turns out to be?"

Harry says, "Maybe our own choice *is* what the universe throws in our path. Say, for example, I chose you, *madeleh*, may I not say the universe sent you to me that night, three years ago, when I heard you read your poems?"

"But you haven't chosen me, Harry, so we can't draw any conclusions from that."

"Haven't I?" Harry says.

I throw him a sardonic look as the door clicks behind me.

CHAPTER THIRTY-SIX

Georgie Phones from PEI

"WHERE THE HELL ARE YOU? Where have you been?"

"I'm in Prince Edward Island. I came here with Alice."

"Jesus Christ, George. I'm absolutely stunned. When did you go? When are you coming home? Why did you go? What's going on?"

"We left ten days ago and I'm leaving for home tomorrow. By train. Be there the day after tomorrow. I'm calling to ask if I can stay with you for a couple of days. I'm coming back earlier than expected and I told Randy he could use my apartment. I don't want to barge in on him."

"Of course you can stay here. Train?"

"Yeah. Alice and I drove, but ..."

"What happened to the car? Did you have an accident?"

"Yes, but not the kind of accident you mean. Alice left a week ago. Don't know where she went. Maybe back in Toronto by now."

"For God's sake, Georgie. What *is* going on?" I repeat.

"I'll tell you about it when I see you."

"I'll pick you up at Union Terminal. Call me when you get there. Give you time to think while you're waiting for me."

"I don't need to think. I've been doing nothing but thinking for a week. The train gets there at 5:20 p.m."

"I'll be there."

That night I lay awake worrying about Georgie. I imagined his contrition for having led Alice to believe ... what ... that she had converted him? That she was so incredibly attractive that he couldn't resist her? What a giddy feeling of power that must have given her— ineluctable desirability even for gay men. Then the reality of his homosexuality: Georgie's disgust with Alice's jelly breasts, her doughy little belly, the expanse of her hips. How awful for both of them. I imagined his humiliating dysfunctionality.

Or what?

CHAPTER THIRTY-SEVEN

Catching Up

AN UNEXPECTED CONSEQUENCE of my book is my loaded calendar. Boyd had called and asked if I would consider lengthening our Saturday night date to commence Saturday morning and continue over Sunday. We could go up to his place in the country and he could show me his favorite spot. I said "Oh," hesitantly, and "Yes" confidently. If I had spoken all the words that named my reaction, they would have included "surprised," "flattered," "eager," "anxious," "worried," "excited." The weekend after that was B&B's benefit. And more Personals replies than I can possibly interview are cramming my mailboxes.

I'm sure an anthropologist or sociologist would trash my book if they learned that I was answering only the most interesting letters. And I'm sure that my assumption is false that a run-of-the-mill letter resembles the person who composed it—the false assumption of a writer *(Sample below). I have to make the cut somewhere, yet it seems so ruthless to totally ignore those hopeful less eloquent seekers. So I reply to them with a gentle let down: I modify the language of a manuscript rejection slip, with which I'm all too well acquainted:

"Dear ——, I would like to have met you, but the number of responses I have received makes that impossible. This is in no way a reflection on your charming letter or your appealing qualities. I wish you success in meeting exactly the person you are looking for." I insert each person's name in the salutation and print the letters out on the computer, so there's no way the recipient can know it is a form letter.

CHAPTER THIRTY-EIGHT

Georgie's Tells Sylvia About
His Trip to PEI

"GOOD LORD, GEORGIE," I blurt, after he stowed his bags and camping gear in the trunk and flopped into the seat next to me. "I remember how hard it was for you to come out of the closet. And what about Randy?

Georgie's laugh sounds like breaking bones: "And telling my parents. Can you imagine even making the attempt: 'Mom and dad, I'm not a fag, after all. I like women. I mean I like both men and women. I guess you'd say I'm half-fagged.'"

The joke resolves for the moment Georgie's dilemma and all the hanging chads of my questions.

We drop the subject until after dinner. Then Georgie thrusts into my hands his recorder with a tape still inside. "Here. I really don't want to sit and talk to you about it. This is what happened. You must have guessed that I was very taken with Alice. During one of our talks she mentioned that she always wanted to go to PEI. I said, me too. Let's go together. She asked if I was kidding and when I realized that I wasn't, we made plans to leave just a few days later for a two-week trip that would include my birthday. Here's the rest. I wouldn't allow anyone but you to hear it, and I really don't want to talk about it after you've listened. Where am I sleeping?"

"Take my room," I say. "I don't mind the pull-out at all."

He doesn't argue, and after he's settled for the night, I pour myself a glass of wine and press play on the machine. Georgie's voice says "It wasn't a terrible week, really—oceans, forests, sand dunes. Then it clicks off. I rewind to the beginning.

Can't believe I'm spilling out my thoughts to a tape recorder. I feel like I'm interviewing myself. But it's faster and easier than writing. Maybe talking to myself out loud will stop the chatter in my head I'm plagued with questions. No answers. Just questions and biting, bitter, thoughts..

Today is July 12. What a hell of a vacation this turned out to be. Exhaust fumes rise from my lungs into my mouth. For two days I've lain on the bed, forcing myself to roll off only when my stomach sends me to the vending machine. Two fucking weeks, less two days, to fill now, on foot, confined to the tip of an island that is still winter in June. Emerson said "A man is about as happy as he makes up his mind to be." Don't know about happy but I'm going to make up my mind to haul my ass out of bed and take a shower and change clothes and eat a real meal. Then I'll find out how to get back to Toronto.

Today is July 17. I haven't done much talking into this thing. I walked, sat staring at the ocean, stretched out on the sand dunes. The beach is mostly deserted, straggle of people, non-stop wind, and sand like powdered terracotta. Farms of potatoes and blueberry bushes grow right down to the ocean.

Two nights I used my sleeping bag after all, laid it down about two miles into the woodland beyond the motel, took only water and a flashlight, no food, no music. There are no large animals on this island, no deer, no fox, or so I've been told, just small furry things like chipmunks and squirrels, a few snakes. I surprised myself by feeling at peace. On PEI the ground itself, some say, gives off peacefulness. There has never been a war here, between white man and white man or white man and Indian or Indian and Indian. The white man, mostly Scottish, just moved in and took over what had been an Indian summer fishing camp.

I always thought of a forest as a leafy tunnel of silence, but at night, in my sleeping bag, I listened to a John Cage symphony— branches creaking, leaves rustling, owls hooting, crickets chirring. There's probably no place on earth that's totally silent. I've recently learned that cricket sounds are made by their wings, not by rubbing their legs together, and not being ignorant about something made me feel more at home. One night a crack like gunfire woke me. Couldn't be a hunter. Stalker movies came to mind. Had Alice tracked me down? But it was only a large branch breaking off somewhere deeper in the dark. The stars were a wonder, thick and low, not much higher than the treetops—all the stars we've pushed so far out of the city skies we thought they were dead.

By the end of my foodless two days, my appetite pounced on me with a lust for lobster, and my motel restaurant provided me with a monster with bulging eyes and huge pincers, yet somehow sweet and tender. I eat all my meals in the motel restaurant. Tonight it's fish and chips and carrots and peas and strawberry-rhubarb pie. Tomorrow morning I'll have my choice of French toast, pancakes, or scrambled eggs. When I'm not eating, I taste exhaust fumes again, as though they're rising from inside myself.

This is July 19. How much of the past is in this moment? Does this very moment, this Now that they tell you to live in, doesn't it contain all the past? Can I liberate this moment from yesterday? Clean it off? Taste only the extraordinary strawberries I picked in the woods, and not the emission from Alice's tailpipe? Can I listen only to the soft mumble of the young couple speaking French at the table next to mine at dinner, blended with the low drone of the radio announcer and the tap of the rain drops. Can I see a bird flying against the steel-grey clouds, and see my hand maneuvering a forkful of food as all part of a time that is happening only now? Time framed like a painting, only itself, without flaw?

How did I get here? I am not able to let the moment be. Can't seem to detach yesterday. When you die you see your life as a series of images, they say, a photo album. But albums turn out to be promo: advertisements for a happy childhood, a popular teen age, an exciting love affair. In the pictures of me as a kid, you could never tell I'd be gay. Be? Was? In albums it was a very good year every year. Here tourists pose with their catch of tuna, back from a day on the *Sea Queen*, run by Captain Hartley Jardine, the motel owner. Captain Hartley catches tuna for his wife to cook and sell to tourists. They both catch tourists, one by the stomach, the other by the pride. Someone asked me to take their picture on the sand dunes.

Then, "Want us to take you?"

"Sure," I said.

"Smile," the girl said.

So I'll have a picture of myself smiling by the ocean. Taste in my mouth invisible.

It always amazed me how there'd be pictures of murdered kids on the day before the murder showing them grinning on their living room sofa, or grinning over the candles on their birthday cake, and the next day, they're dead. Drowned, or shot, or smothered.

The smiling anglers stand beside the smiling marlin. There's no desperate marlin wrenching, straining, swimming madly away with the hook in its mouth.

The scale says 980 pounds. A sign is pinned to the fish itself or to a blackboard set up between the catcher and the caught:

Angler: Beverly Dorman

Vessel: *The Lucky Strike*

Date: July 21, 2007

Pounds: 980

The area of pier beneath the fish's head where it hangs is dark and slimy red, lipstick red, with blotchy edges, like a smudged kiss. Some of the photos are of sunsets and birds flying across clouds, across streaks of gold and orange.

Half the album is still blank.

What am I? Am I queer? Am I straight. Do I have to declare myself? Why can't I say this is my blue period, this is my cubist period, this is my abstract expressionism period. Everything is a period. For never, never did I expect ten days ago, to be sitting here on my twenty-ninth birthday in a diner behind a ten-unit motel on the northeast tip of an island in the Atlantic, watching the ocean, and with rain pouring down the reflection of my face in the window.

Today is July 24. I'm going to cut my adventure short by a couple of days. I'll hop a bus to Charlottetown. Then Via Rail from there to Montreal and from Montreal to Toronto. Better than the hassle of flying and the sudden transition from where you were to where you're going. The train will be good. Comforting. A different kind of space. A plane is no space—limbo.

It wasn't easy for me to come out of the closet. Now do I go back in? Is there a closet for the reconverted? For fallen away homosexuals? Am I going to go in one closet and out the other? Revolving closet doors like a farce?"

July 25. Talking to this tape actually has brought me some relief, but it hasn't helped me understand. Maybe if I go over the whole trip, step by step.

The friction began before we pulled away from the curb in front of my apartment. We had agreed to one medium-sized suitcase each—all that could fit into the hatch of her Civic. We had drawn lots for whose car we would use, and agreed to split expenses down the middle. The back seat would be taken up with sleeping bags and the camping equipment I was bringing. We thought it would be fun to sleep under the stars some nights, something I hadn't done since I was a kid, and Alice had never done. I imagined an evergreen forest, the scent of pine needles, the sound of a brook. Lyrical.

I was waiting on the curb when she pulled up to my apartment, all smiles, ready to roll. I hadn't been so excited about a trip to anywhere for a long time. When she opened the hatch, I was confronted with a suitcase only slightly smaller than a steamer trunk. My smile turned to "Shit! Where am I supposed to put this?"

"Oh, George," she said, still smiling, "Can't your case fit in there?"

"It's a suitcase," I said, "not a briefcase."

" 'Oh, sorry,' she said. 'Put it in the back seat with the camping stuff,' which I did, though now most of the rear window was blocked. There wouldn't be room for the carton of Prince Edward Island organic strawberry preserve and crate of frozen lobsters, but my budget was so tight, I thought, it was probably just as well.

I never feel that my travels have begun until I'm past everything that's familiar. It took about twenty minutes, and by then I was happy and excited again. We were taking I-90 through New York and she said she would love to stop the night at the Women's Freedom Enclave in Seneca Falls, but men weren't allowed.

I said, sure. I'd get a motel near by and not to worry; I knew how to amuse myself. I don't know what she took that to mean.

The next day, when I picked her up, she didn't ask any questions. Not a query about where I'd stayed or what I'd done, as though I had done something she felt I would be embarrassed to talk about.

At breakfast in one of the little towns off the highway, everything seemed fine. We had two more days on the road, after the Women's thing, driving I-95 through Massachusetts, branching into Route 1 into Maine and New Brunswick, finally crossing Confederation Bridge to PEI and up to Campbell's Cove near North Point.

Our second night on the road, we stopped at four motels. All booked. So we spelled each other and napped and drove right through to the next afternoon.

The brochures hadn't lied about PEI. It was green enough to share the title "Emerald" with Ireland. Every direction we turned we saw water and something I had never seen—farms that didn't stop until they reached the ocean. This island *felt* like an island, a piece of land tethered to the sea bottom.

An uncle had left Alice a strip of land with ocean frontage in Fairfield, near Campbell's Cove, facing out toward the *Îlles-de-la-Madeleine*. She said, 'I was waiting for the right person to see it with.'

We had reservations at a small motel on an isthmus of land, frequented mostly by deep-sea fishermen, and planned to arrive about sundown. The reservation was for one room. I had been aroused, I think, from our first meeting. We hadn't done anything. In fact hardly touched.

Our first whole day on the road after Seneca Falls was light-hearted. We were annoyed with each other only a couple of times, mildly, and I can't even remember what about—once I think she asked something about the way she wore her hair, and my answer made her grumpy enough to remove her hand from my thigh for the next couple of hours. But those couple of off-key moments didn't spill into our first night together. It was the kind you see in movies, with the lovers undressing each other and devouring whatever part presented itself to their lips. But we weren't imitating the movies. We didn't do the panting, screaming, frenzied mutual undressing that movies and TV have made to seem obligatory. It all came bubbling up naturally, like uncorked champagne.

The next day, we drove on in the afterglow of the night before. We kept our hands on each other's thighs or higher. At about four o'clock in the afternoon, with only three hours left to drive to the Seafarer Motel, she brought up, once again, her marriage, and complained once again about her former husband's treatment of her. In an offhand way, I said, "Well, it takes two to tango." My comment infuriated her. Infuriated. She fell into a frozen, enraged silence. 'I'm sorry,' I apologized. 'I didn't mean to hurt your feelings.'

"So!" she said. "You think it was my fault that we got a divorce, my failure."

"No." I defended myself. "'I was only generalizing. I only meant that it's not one person's fault. It's interaction, don't you think? I was only stating a psychological truism.'" I continued to try to extricate myself: " 'But there are always exceptions. Your situation sounds like an exception.'" "She wouldn't let me off the hook, 'So you think it *was* my fault,' she said, and didn't say another word for the rest of the trip. She kept her hands to herself and her eyes fixed on the road. When I tried to talk to her, she said, 'George, I'm really not in the mood to talk.'

I didn't press it. I was sure the tension would dissolve by the time we got to the motel. After all, the sky was blue, the fields glowed with every color of lupine and you could smell bayberry bushes for miles. We would soon be smiling at each other again, I thought.

When we got to the motel we both went in to register and get the key. We both returned to the car and she backed into the allotted space in front of our room. She still didn't say a word, but her shoulders seemed relaxed and her face was a mask of what I thought was tranquility. We both got out of the car to unpack. She removed my suitcase from the back seat and placed it on the ground. I removed my sleeping bag and camping stuff. Great, I thought. She's helping me unload, so she's over whatever it was that bothered her.

Then, she got back into the car and drove away.

Unbelievable. She just drove away. No wave, no word, no accusation, no explanation. Just drove off. I expected to see her car pause down the road, and U-turn back around. When it didn't, I thought she would stew for a while and cool off, or have a drink at some wayside bar and reconsider. Yet something about the rear end of her car looked very final. I watched until it disappeared far down the road. Then I stared at the exhaust from her tailpipe hang in the air a few seconds longer.

I'll never forget that exhaust, appearing behind the car, then slowly disappearing. Then the whole automobile seemed to vaporize in space like a gray ghost.

I lay down in this dismal little backwater motel, filled with hatred for her, though at that point I still expected a car to shuffle into the space outside and to hear a knock at the door. I thought she might stay at a B&B in Charlottetown. She'd get up at 7:00 or 8:00 and she'd be back here at about 10:00.

It wasn't a terrible week, really—oceans, forests, sand dunes.

I stayed up most of the night, first listening to the tape and then being almost as perturbed as Georgie had been.

The next morning, it was strange meeting Georgie in my kitchen. He was just staring out the window. I poured myself some coffee, and to break the silence, I actually began to talk about the weather. It took a huge effort to refrain from bringing up the only thing I was interested in. But Georgie had let me into his most private thoughts and asked me not to question him. I didn't.

He would probably appreciate having my apartment to himself, while I was away with Boyd over the next two days.

CHAPTER THIRTY-NINE

My One Night Weekend

HE PICKED ME UP AT EIGHT on Saturday morning. The birds were in full operatic mode, the sun shone at high beam; happy the affair the sun shines on today. *Was* this an affair or just a sleepover?

Boyd knew the scenic routes, interesting wayside shops and rural culinary gems. We stopped at the home studio of a ceramicist, a middle-aged, plump, frizzy-haired woman who greeted him with an enthusiastic, "Boyd, dear! It has been a long time. A long winter. It seems to me you haven't been around since the frost was on the pumpkin."

"I know," he says, bending over to kiss her. "Busy." And between that and his next words, I wondered how many new 'himselves' he had discovered up here.

"Martha, this is my friend, Sylvia. She's a writer. Writing a book about Personals ads and the people who indulge in them."

"Are you up to that game again, Boyd?"

"Never stopped," he says. And turns to me, "Martha knows everything about me. And I couldn't forget about her even if I wanted to because her creations look at me from several rooms in my house."

Literally look at him, I found, as she showed me around her studio. Eyes were a recurring motif in her work. Some eyes were patterned in the glaze, some inscribed into the clay, some raised. They reminded me of the designs in Judy Chicago's vaginal dinner plates or Georgia O'Keefe's flowers. To me, her work looked museum quality. I might have known that Boyd would have exquisite taste. It was one of the few times I wished I had deeper pockets. Then I remembered what Rock said, "I want them all, so I go to a museum." I lingered over a small bowl, completely closed up except for a hole just large enough for the stem of one flower, and which, when I turned it this way and that, presented the faintest suggestion of one wide-open eye. It's faintly blue, luminescent color looked as though a candle was flickering inside.

"She'll have this one," Boyd says to Martha.

"No! No! Not at all!" I say, feeling heat rise to my face.

"Sylvia, really. It's nothing."

"Absolutely not." I say.

"Will you accept it from me?" Martha asks. "I would really like to give a friend of Boyd's a small memento."

I didn't know what to say. To continue to refuse seemed terribly petty and more grasping than to accept it.

"Thank you," I say. "I'll treasure it."

At about one o'clock we stopped for lunch at another place where Boyd is greeted with warm familiarity. How many women had he brought up to his special place? How many had Martha courted for him with small round pots with single flower openings? During our interview he had mentioned only one. Then he must come here frequently with his family or alone.

This time I am introduced to Hsue, and we eat Chinese delicacies that one rarely finds in the city, let alone on a country road. About an hour after lunch we arrived at Boyd's cottage—a modest three bedroom with large windows and stone floors, furnished in wicker and glowing with cleanliness. Obviously someone had been in to polish floors and squeegee windows.

I was very nervous. He showed me to the bedroom and closed the door as he left. I didn't know what I was supposed to do in the bedroom. I was wearing the clothes I intended to wear that night, so my overnight case contained only a robe, toiletries, and a change for tomorrow of the same sort of thing I was wearing today, only chinos instead of jeans. So I washed my face, brushed my teeth, and combed my hair. I was standing in the middle of the room, still not knowing what to do, when Boyd entered without knocking. He stepped over to me and began removing my clothes.

"This will make you feel more at home," he says.

Afterward, I say, "I'd like to see the place you find so beautiful."

He sighs deeply. "All right."

We walked out into that time of day that passes between the setting of the sun and the rising of evening—half the world dappled rosy and gold and half fading to pale silver. Up a small hill so steep that Boyd extends a hand to help pull me up. At the top, the sun is still radiant and fields and fields of wild flowers stretch toward low mountains.

"It *is* beautiful," I say.

"Look to your left," he says.

I turn my head and catch my breath. Totally unexpectedly there appears a narrow river of running water, perfectly clear, gently churning over stones, enclosed by steep green banks, and shaded by tall cypress. A footbridge spans the water, and here the late low glimmer of the sun shines luminously stippled over everything. I feel the presence, surely there was a presence, of something divine. I whisper, "It is wonderful." A turn of the head brought two worlds together, one sunny and vividly colored and expansive—land of the sun god; the other mysterious and dark, seductively murmuring—land of the god of twilight.

We stood silently for quite a long time, until Boyd put his arm around me and we walked back to the cottage.

"I'm sorry to disappoint you," I say with mock flippancy, "but I don't think I'm going to help you see it in a different way. I can only agree that it must be your favorite spot on earth." His arm around me tightened.

Apparently Boyd had engaged not only a house-cleaner but a cook; and dinner had been laid out in the refrigerator, needing only to be heated. After dinner as we sipped cordials I couldn't stop myself from talking about what I had been thinking about, even though, since I was not here in my role as writer/interviewer, I felt I was prying. I had wondered if he had ever been caught. I didn't think so, since he was still doing it. And I wondered if he had ever fallen in love with a Person and found it painful to break off. And I was thinking that Personals did not substitute for destiny or fate, but really expanded destiny's scope. Everything still continued to 'just happen.' One *decided* to step into many Personals ads just as one decided to step into the crowded room. Beyond that initial act, fate stepped in.

"When we say half of me likes that or half of me thinks that, I wonder what the other half is thinking or feeling?"

He chuckles. "Sylvia, you wonder about strange things. Well, what *is* the other half of you thinking?"

"I am wondering how often? How many? I am wondering if you have ever been caught. You said the possibility of being caught frightened you. I'm wondering if you have ever fallen in love with a Personals. I'm wondering if you know that your serial Personals games is rather ruthless, using women to enrich your concept of yourself."

I knew immediately that I had just ruined the weekend. It could not be salvaged from this barrage.

"And what do you think you are doing, writing your book?" he retorts. "Aren't you using women and men and whoever comes for your own purpose? Isn't your book a ruthless enterprise? And no," he says, unmistakably setting me straight, "I have never fallen in love with *any* woman since I married my wife. Nor will I ever. I told you, my wife suits me perfectly and I appreciate and enjoy family life. I will never change that."

"But you risk it."

"Not really. Not emotionally."

I had already ruined the night, so I thought I might as well go on with my interrogation as long as he was willing to respond. Indeed, I could hardly stop myself.

"But you don't sound as though you're in love with your wife."

"Yes. I love my wife."

"But not *in* love." I felt naively romantic making the distinction I had often felt was silly.

"Yes to that, too. I married her because I fell in love with her. But she is not the one who prevents me from falling in love with someone else. She is not the woman who prevents me from leaving her for another woman."

He then went on to tell me the strangest reason I have ever

heard for not leaving one's wife. When he was very young, twenty-two and twenty-three, Boyd was passionately, irreversibly, profoundly in love with a young woman—his Great Love. In his rising up and his lying down, his going out and his coming in, she was the fulcrum upon which his world turned. They were together for almost two years. But he couldn't have her, couldn't keep her. He didn't tell me why they broke apart. It took a long time—years — before the pain wore off sufficiently to look at another woman. Then he fell quietly in love with his wife. The Great Love was the savior of his marriage. The Great Love kept him faithful to his wife, not sexually faithful, but faithful to their bond. His wife was Second Best and there was no reason to switch to third best or fourth best. Only the Great Love was better than his wife, and since she was unattainable, even if still alive, she was out of reach, and now buried under the rubble of many years. Fidelity to *that* love is what kept him faithful to his wife.

"No one can supplant her," Boyd says, "so I am not looking for someone to do the impossible, and I am content with Second Best. That is not an insignificant category," he says, "Imagine being second best in the world at anything."

Boyd did not come into my room again, and early on Sunday morning we drove home, in quite an affable mood. Our mutual enticement had simply faded into pleasantness.

CHAPTER FORTY

Pre-Party

THE FOLLOWING SATURDAY, I deliberated about taking a cab to B&B's house, but there seemed no reason to, since I was dressed in jeans and shirt and carried no luggage. I would be returning home in the same clothes I was now wearing, having spent the intervening hours in couture I could never afford. I did carry panty hose and shoes in my shoulder bag, both of which turned out to be inappropriate. Harry would arrive at nine, and I prayed that he would not be clothed in his professorial "dress" outfit of turtleneck and tweed jacket with leather elbows. His work outfit was jeans with sweater in the winter and jeans with polo in the summer.

On the subway and then the bus I fought down the feeling that I was back at university and on my way to a lavish party as one of the servers for the Sous Chef Catering Company to tote trays of bite-sized gourmet nibbles and Champagne.

Blythe herself opened the door, a nice gesture I thought, rather than having me formally shown in by a maid. I was stunned by the place. Not that I hadn't visited large, splendid houses before, but not being journalist to the rich and famous I had never entered a version of Buckingham Palace. My mouth did not fall agape, but that it was agape showed in my eyes.

"Be it ever so humble," Blythe says, not pretending not to notice the impression it made on me. She hugs me and asks if I wanted coffee or tea or anything. I decline and we climb the stairs to her suite.

"We have plenty of time," she says, "to relax and have fun and indulge ourselves. First, let's find you a dress."

Her clothes closet is a closet in the same way that a forty-room mansion in the Hamptons is a cottage. She indicates one section that she refers to as "Not yet worn in Toronto." For some reason, I had expected to be wearing a long gown.

"Tonight is very informal," she says. "Street length." And I recall that the invitation Harry received said nothing about black tie.

I feel like I am on a shopping spree at Bergdorfs. I leaf through the rack of Not-yet-worn-in-Toronto clothes and chose a dress of many colors—a rainbow of layers of sheer floating chiffon that seemed unmade by human hands.

"Isn't it gorgeous? It will be charming on you." Blythe says, "This is what I'll be wearing," taking a dress from the rack of Not-yet-worn-anywhere. It is black, sleeveless, décolleté, perfectly plain, with a flounce at the hemline, and I understand that she is suggesting I choose something black. I rehang the fairy tale garment and leaf through the dresses again, now thoroughly unsure of myself.

"I don't think this is my type," I say, holding a dress in front of my body. "What do you think?"

"Perfect. You'll be stunning. Try it on. Our tailor stands ready for any nip or tuck."

But he wasn't needed. The slim black dress with the tight long sleeves, with gathers drawn snugly around the hip, asymmetrically clinched with a large rhinestone ornament, fits perfectly.

"You'll wear no jewelry," Blythe instructs, except for earrings. You'll wear my long diamond drops. Now for shoes."

"I brought shoes. I don't know why, but I thought we would be wearing long gowns. I'm sure they're not right."

"They're very pretty," she manages to say, "but you're right, not for this dress. Come, look at these."

She shows me to a wall shelved with shoes enough to make her eligible to be First Lady of the Philippines.

"Please, nothing made for women with one toe." I say.

"No. Anyway those are passé. Toes a bit rounded now. How do you feel about very high heels?"

"I would feel terrible about them if I had to run for a bus, but I think I can manage tonight. If you help me down the stairs."

The shoes fit as perfectly as my own. Better. My own with an $800 upgrade.

"Amazing," she says. "You could be my clone." She hurries to cover what could be an insult, "Size-wise I mean. Let's see, it's three o'clock. Guests will begin to arrive at nine. I could stand a nap for about an hour. Could you? Or you could read. Should we do that first, then a massage or visa versa? Then we'll shower, do nails, hair, and makeup."

I begin reading on the chaise in the guest room, but quickly fall asleep. At five-thirty Blythe's knock at the door wakes me. Of course the towels are lush, the robe is lush, and the soap is creamy and unscented.

The manicurist performs both manicure and pedicure. The shoes I'll be wearing don't reveal toes, but apparently in Blythe's house one set of nails can't be conceived of without the other. Then the makeup artist takes over. And finally, the hairdresser.

At eight-forty-five Blythe comes into my room to pick me up and we descend the stairway together.

Barry is already in the living room. "My!" he says. "Two of you is too much for one man's eyes."

CHAPTER FORTY-ONE

The Benefit Party

THIS IS NOT A LANDSCAPE I'm used to. Harry arrives with the punctual guests at 9:00, having displayed his invitation to the parking attendant and again at the door.

All evening just glimpsing him across the room makes me feel secure. If I needed to I could go up and stand next to him. He seems to be talking to a lot of people. He seems always to be at the center of movable little clutches of conversation, with women looking up at him admiringly. He does look good in his navy jacket and white shirt opened at the neck, as good as any of the other men, all in the same uniform. How did he know not to come in his V-necked sweater and tie or his navy blue suit?

Everyone looks so happy—smiling and laughing as though a photographer had just instructed, "Cheese." Except me. When the muscles in my face tire of stretching into a smile, they fall into their usual expression—serious? Dour? Hard to know what your usual expression is; when you look into a mirror you assume a face to meet the face you meet.

Everyone looks polished, tanned, taken care of. Even me, as a result of the magicians at Blythe's court.

I find myself fall into an unhealthy habit I've formed lately of applying statistics to groups of people I see. I could be sitting in a concert audience of 500 and I scan the crowd and say to myself, there are ten pedophiles in this audience and there are twenty rapists and there are twenty men who abuse their wives. All listening to Mozart. Horrible thought. Maybe there is an overlap; the same twenty who are rapists are also the ones who abuse their wives. That would reduce the total. And there are fifty women who have been molested as children, sitting in this concert hall right now, in their silk dresses and latest hair dos. And all these women look like everyone else in the audience; they smile and laugh and exit with their hands in the crook of their husband's arm. And during the intermission the rapists and wife beaters and grown-up molested little girls mill around and greet others and behave charmingly.

Or I could be walking down Bloor Street or Bay Street and think, thirty to forty percent of you people I'm passing on the sidewalk are bankrupting your companies or stealing from unimportant folks like me, or corrupting the media and publishing houses and the book marketing business. But you look absolutely normal, like everyone else. You do not look unsavory like the man sitting on the sidewalk with his cap extended for small change. You do not look castoff like the woman dressed in layers of all the clothing she owns, pushing all her earthly goods in a shopping cart. When I was very little I remember seeing people acting crazy, wailing in the street, mumbling to themselves or cursing out loud. You do not look or act like them. It is frightening to me how you can't tell a rotten person from a good one. You should be able to smell them— sulfurish, like a spoiled egg. They should wear a white hood or a scarlet K on their upper arm.

Now, at B&B's party I'm scanning the upper upper strata of society, moving among the backdrop of huge bouquets of cut flowers, and wondering which of them cheated on their spouses. All? How many cheated on their income tax? All? How many cared about Third World children who worked twelve hours a day in their offshore companies? How many traveled to Thailand or South America to have sex with children? And I wondered—if each of the women here tonight donated the price of the new ball gown she will purchase for the next fundraiser, added to the cost of the food and drink served at the fundraiser, if that wouldn't raise more money than the pledged contributions. To be fair, probably not. Some of these people donate millions.

I'm deep into this depressing train of thought when I find Harry standing beside me.

"Are you writing a poem?"

"Harry, hey!" I say, embarrassed that he had found me standing alone like an outsider. "Go!" I say, " Mingle! You're cramping my style," and I help myself to a second glass of champagne from the tray of a roving server, and move into the heat of the party. One more glass would sweep me from the doldrums and open my ears to the laughter and good-humored conversation. Two more glasses and I would join in and have fun.

I'm sipping my fourth glass as I walk toward the group which is dancing near the musicians, and someone grabs me around the waist and twirls me toward the dancers. I had been wondering if I could perambulate on the stiletto heels, let alone dance, but I manage.

"Scott," he says. "Scott Bigelow."

"I'm Sylvia Weisler."

"New in town?"

"No. Just new at B&B's"

He looks puzzled, then gets the initials. "They *are* rather a sweet liquor, aren't they?"

"I'm rather a new friend," I say.

"I'm sure I'll be grateful to them," he says. "Am already."

We dance one after another, remaining on the dance floor between numbers, until dinner is served at 11:00. I had caught glimpses of Harry on the dance floor. Now he appears and takes me by the elbow.

"Oh, Harry. This is Scott. Scott Bigelow. Scott this is Harry Sympler."

"Oh," Scott says. "Sympler Books?"

"Yes."

"Good stuff," Scott says.

"Thanks," Harry says. "Sylvie, our table is over there."

Dinner is a quartet of buffets at four stations offering cuisine from the four corners of the world—Japanese, Italian, French, American South—with a consort of wines and piano music. "I hope you have *one* empty space on your dance card," Harry says, when the combo starts to play again.

"Of course," I say, surprised by his sarcasm.

We dance two and return to our table. Scott comes up and twirls his hand as an invitation to dance again.

"The spirit is willing," I say, shaking my head no.

"I look forward to next time," he says to me, and goodnight to both of us.

I couldn't leave with Harry because I had to change back into my own clothes. Just the opposite of a butterfly, I thought, as I unobtrusively waited for the last guests to leave. After I changed back into my jeans, Blythe said, "I hope you had a good time—a *very* good time—because I would love for you to join us on our boat for a short cruise. Just a couple of days. Can you do lunch tomorrow? I'll tell you all about it."

I was driven home in the B&B limo.

CHAPTER FORTY-TWO

GA Reflects

OUR AUTHOR STOPPED in the other day to tell me about some of her interviews and particularly, I believe, to talk about her weekend with Boyd and the party at Blythe and Barron's. She uses me, you see, to get her muddled thoughts out of the cave and into the light.

As to the former, I cautioned her to beware of stories that sound like chick-lit or the male version thereof, prick lit. Stories in which, for example, Older Rich Husband has a Beautiful Second Wife and a Young, Handsome Brother with whom BSW falls into requited love. YHB is poor, but sure enough ORH dies, leaving YHB his estate (except for the gratuity that went to First Wife) and it is his duty, by Biblical injunction, to marry BSW.

The latter subject is what arrested and alarmed me. She talked on and on about the elegance and opulence of the place and the people, not forgetting to mention Scott (surely someone's YHB). I was alarmed that even one day's exposure to life at the top of the top could disturb her satisfaction with her own life—home-done fingernails, "some short, some long, and too pointy," and her toenails, "trimmed by being picked at and never glossed or colored. Never!" she complained.

You know by now that our heroine is forthright, empathetic, intelligent, and possessed of a wide democracy of spirit. But rather naïve. In fact surprisingly naïve in one no longer quite young. But she is inclined to impulsiveness, as only the naïve can be, and to following her nose in directions that wisdom would pull the other way. Most frightening to me, who is very fond of her, is her lack of self-knowledge. She constantly confuses her ostensible motives—ideas she picked up from books (a common failure among writers) with her real motives.

Our hero, Harry, on the other hand, though scarcely older, is wise, insightful, kind, and not *imposing*, in both meanings of that word.

For my part, I didn't say much, but taking the conversation in quite a different direction, I confessed that her stories about Rock had captured my interest and I asked Sylvia if she would mind if I met with her.

"Gladwell, you're kidding!" she yelped as her eyebrows shot to her hairline.

"No, Sylvie. Nothing like that. There's a question I've been turning over in my mind since you began writing this book, and from what I've gleaned from your descriptions of her, she seems intelligent and forthcoming. There's something I'd like her opinion about."

"Descartes? Spinosza? James Joyce?" she teased.

"On a part of the male anatomy."

CHAPTER FORTY-THREE

Rock's News

"Hey, girl." Rock meets me at the door of Tony's bar as though it is her home. Tony makes a hi-five gesture in the air.

Rock's voice is cheerful, but she looks a little tired. She leads the way to our usual booth, where she has a pad of legal paper and a pen spread out.

"Whenever I see you, Rock, I think, What's a good Jewish woman doing sitting around observing bar hounds and writing neighborhood porn, when she should be home making matzo balls."

"Fine one to talk. You should be home taking care of babies instead of peeping into people's love affairs, or lack thereof. This is my place of employment. I hustle here. You'd be surprised how many regulars I have, and they pay for just words, no pictures. Shows intelligence, I say. And it's fun to write porn. You should try it. I'm amazed how creative I am. Each story is different. Things I never actually did. Kind of like porn sci-fi without the aliens—all fantasy."

"Sublimation?" I ask. "Since Tina left?"

"You know I was writing this stuff long before she arrived. But that's what I called to tell you about. I heard from her! I saw her!"

I'm both eager to hear and disappointed that my book would not be credited with the reunion.

"Those ads we placed worked! One of her friends saw them and called her, and she called me. Phoned. I cried as soon as I heard her voice. All I could manage to say was 'Yes,' when she asked if she could come over."

Rock tells me that that between the phone call and Tina's arrival her hearing became as acute and intense as a new mother's listening for the breathing of her baby in the next room. She was certain she would hear the car door close a block away, and hear Tina's footstep over the noise of the traffic.

"I could hardly make it to the door when her knock finally came. She said, 'Hello, Rock.' I couldn't move either out of the doorway or toward her, like my feet were nailed to the floor. It was raining and she was wet. Why is it always raining when something important happens, like funerals and trains leaving the station? I shook myself out of my paralysis and took her wet raincoat—one of those plastic things with a hood. And then she hugged me, and I knew everything was over except the love. She gave me a friendship hug, with three little pats on the back. You know, lovers' hugs never include pats."

"Oh," I say, and wait for her to go on.

"Well. She is gone. She was in my arms but she is gone from me for good. She's married. And she's pregnant. And I love her anyway." I had so securely situated Tina in my mind as a languishing lesbian that I could hardly assimilate this.

"Oh," I say again.

"She didn't even go to a shrink. She had an epiphany."

"An epiphany about being a lesbian?"

"No. An epiphany about the danger of men. I mean the non-danger of men."

And then Rock spills out the story. "This man she married is the brother of a friend. Tina was a houseguest one weekend—a large house with lots of bedrooms. She opened the wrong door and walked into the brother's bedroom by mistake one afternoon. It was a hot summer day—Fourth of July weekend—and he was lying on his back on his bed stark naked and had a straight up boner.

"She fought with her impulse to flee, as always, and succeeded, because the owner of the boner was harmlessly sleeping. Tina stood in the doorway and had a mental conversation with it in which it reassured her she had nothing to fear from it. I imagine the conversation going something like Penis talking to Tina like Balaam's Ass; 'What have I done to you, that you run from me all these times?' And Tina says, 'Because you have frightened me. I wish I had a sword in my hand, for then I would kill you.' And the penis says to Tina, 'Am I not your friend that you could ride upon. Did I ever do you harm?'

134

"When the conversation was over (the brother, Mitch, sleeping peacefully the whole time,) she stepped out of the bedroom, not only cured but madly in love with Mitchell. It was love at first sight."

"Wonderful!" I cry. "Amazing."

"Well," Rock says. "Not all together wonderful. She found her heart and she lost her feet. She's not running at all anymore. She's coaching a women's track team. That man who terrified her when she was a kid by exposing his organ, was the wings beneath her feet."

"Oh," I say again, and immediately think of a chapter for my book, entitled 'The Wound and the Wings.'

After a long pause in which I try to assimilate all the ramifications of this story, I ask, "Are you going to see her again?"

"Yeah. Can you believe she wants me to be her kid's godmother? Can you imagine a Jewish, lesbian godmother who used to be the lover of the mother? If it's a girl, she's going to name her Raquel, my given name. And it it's a boy, Peter—the rock Jesus built his ministry on. Can you believe it?"

"What a story, Rock," I say. "It's a mind blower. Rock, are you happy or sad?"

"I don't know. I don't know what I am."

Another long silence, and Tony answers my lifted hand signal. We needed something stronger than beer. "Two double shots," I say, "and beer chasers."

The air of Tony's Bar & Grill is lambent with images of sleeping Mitch with a hard-on, pregnant Tina, and imminent births. Rock gives her body a little shake, like a Labrador retriever climbing out of a pond. "I'm thinking about my porn writing," she says. "I've figured out why so many more men than women write science fiction. It's because men's babies appear suddenly, out of nowhere. They may as well have popped out of a drainpipe. Only a man could have invented the story of baby delivery by stork. He puts his cock into something, moves it around, takes it out and goes away. Nine months later someone brings him a baby and tells him it's his. During the whole nine months, while the woman's body is trans-figured to something she doesn't recognize as herself, and she can't

135

stop thinking about the man who caused this physiological enormity, nothing at all is happening to him. He's off playing golf. He can hardly remember the night of the cock, and there's nothing that makes that particular cocknight different from other similar nights. Pure Sc-Fi."

"That reminds me Rock, my friend Gladwell Alcox would like to meet you. He says he's been pondering a question—something about men's relationship with their private part—that he thinks you might shed some light on."

"I don't know whether to be honored or insulted, but sure, I'll meet with him. Do you want to set it up?

CHAPTER FORTY-FOUR

How's the Book Coming?

ONE OF THE PERKS of publishing with a small house is that you actually get to talk to the publisher. Of course as friends, Harry and I talk all the time. So his invitation to lunch to discuss the book stamped this meeting as more formal and official than a casual book-biz chat, increasing the anxiety I already felt about my slow progress.

"Are you inviting Georgie?"

"Should I?"

I say, "I've written up all his interviews, but he always has interesting asides. If you don't mind."

"I'll phone him."

"Meet at the deli?" I ask, trying to confirm our close friendship by predicting where he would want to go.

"No," he says. "The Zendo, a Japanese fusion that opened on Collins."

"Twelve-thirty, as usual?"

"No." He corrects my assumption again. "I thought I'd pick you up at noon. That will give us time to talk alone on the way to the restaurant, before Georgie joins us."

"I won't be coming from home," I say, unexpectedly flustered. "In fact, I'm meeting a Person at 10:30 for coffee."

"All right," Harry says, somewhat irritably. " See you and George at the restaurant at 12:30."

That night I dream my recurring dream about sitting in a movie theater with Harry, watching a romantic flick. He says, as he always does, "There's no one I'd rather witness this movie with than you."

"Witness?" I echo. "Like the movie is on trial?"

He says, "Like we're going to have to report every detail of what we see."

"Report to who?" I ask.

Then a woman with a wide-brimmed hat and a very tall man sit down in front of us and we can no longer see the screen. We get up to leave and I realize we've been at a matinee, as bright daylight blinds us when we emerge from the dark theater, and the dream dissolves in a luminous blur.

The next day at lunch I tell Harry that the book was taking longer than I thought. We had been shooting for a manuscript completion date of November, and a spring publication date.

"Probably six months longer," I admit, "I've just been so busy."

"Busy with the book?"

"With things that grew out of the book. Not directly related." If my explanation made Harry think of B&B's party and wonder if I was busy with more of the same, he wouldn't be far off. Neither would he inquire. He would wait for me to elucidate.

Georgie rescues the awkward moment by mentioning his vacation with one of the women he interviewed. Of course I hadn't told Harry about this extension of Georgie's interviewer function and he is visibly astonished.

"The interview will be in the book?"

"Yes," I respond for Georgie, "but not the rest of it. Not the vacation."

Georgie doesn't contribute anything more about "the rest of it," and Harry, sensitive and tactful, as always, changes the subject.

"I would love to meet the woman," I say, "but Georgie probably wouldn't condone it."

"You're absolutely right," Georgie says with unusual sharpness. "No reason to. You have the book interview in full. There's nothing more you need to know."

I was sure he regretted allowing me to listen to the tape, that revealed so much.

"Tell me about your interview this morning," Harry says to me.

"Pretty much run-of-the-mill. Probably won't use it. But I had a very unusual interview yesterday. This woman met a man through Personals that she feels she keeps meeting in various life times."

"Uh oh," Harry and Georgie say in unison.

"She let me tape it and I have my recorder right here from my interview this morning. Want to hear it?"

The tape played quietly, much more quietly than the periodic cell phone rings around us and overly loud voices that answered them.

"I have been with him for two years this time," the tape recorder says. Her voice is soft and contains a natural vibrato or else is tremulous with emotion. "Somewhere during these two years an image began to form in my mind. The image was vague at first. Then it became sharper and sharper like a slide brought into focus. I began to believe that he and I had first met eons ago. The image was set in Paleolithic time, in Neanderthal time.

"I did not look as I look now. I was blonde, very fair. My hair was very long, very silky. My skin was very white. I cannot identify my clothing when I first appear, something light and thin. The image is faint, but I know it was very different from the kind of shift made of animal skin that I wore later. Still later I see myself as filthy and my garment shredded. I am bruised. I stumble when I try to walk. I am hungry. And I am engulfed in a terrible anguish. I had been exiled from the tribe when the male who was my protector discarded me. I was overcome by a pain of soul so total that when I am finally torn apart by ... I don't know whether by animals or humans, I submit to my ending with numbed relief."

Harry is shakings his head in disbelief and looking at the tape recorder with combined astonishment and aversion.

"I didn't expect this book to contain such bizarre stories. I thought it would give us glimpses into the behavior of normal people."

"Maybe they *are* normal," Georgie says in a tone that is almost defiant.

I press the play key again.

The soft voice continues, "And he does not look as he does now. He was then much broader and more muscular, a massive face, though with high cheekbones as it is now, hair a tangle, countenance wild. But I know it is the same man I am with now. And I know that I had come from a different place, a different country, than the one in which I found myself. I was a stranger in a strange land, lost and starving. He rescued me, took me in. I was unlike anyone in his tribe—besides my fair hair and skin, I was far more delicate, smaller boned and finely chiseled. I could not have survived except by his care and custody. Even under his protection I endured sly pokes and insults and ferocious glances.

"But I was his charm and his pleasure. He never tired of looking at me and touching me. He looked and looked and touched and touched. I was his fascination, his obsession and he was my life, literally and figuratively. Then he who had answered every whim turned to stone and would not permit me to remain at his side. Thus the ending that I have described to you.

"I do not know why he turned away from me, and nothing that occurred in the eons since then—all the lives that reunited us, has supplied an answer. Maybe this life will.

"The Personals ad I placed wasn't just an ad, you see, it was the way destiny operated in current time. So I'm stuck you see. I cannot liberate myself from him."

My voice comes on the tape. "Does he see it that way too?"

"No. He becomes extremely impatient, even irate, when I talk about our previous lives. If he doesn't remember, I know that the time will come when he casts me off again. Maybe that's destiny too—the way our inseparable bond is tested until, some day—it *must* happen some day—he sees that we are the two halves of the whole that mythology speaks of."

The recorder clicks off.

"Jeeze," Georgie says.

"My god," Harry says. "The book is beginning to worry me. You'd better start answering the run-of-the-mill letters."

"That's my problem," I say. "Run-of-the-mill stories won't make a book, and the others are so weird or the participants are so non-average that I wonder if the reader will believe them. I sometimes don't believe them, but I have the advantage of observing facial expressions and body language."

"I guess we have no choice but to believe them." Harry says.

"Isn't it your job to make the mundane interesting?" Georgie says.

CHAPTER FORTY-FIVE

Scene in which Professor Alcox
Meets Rock

"YOU'RE VERY MUCH as I imagined you," Rock says.

"And you're younger than I imagined you," I reply. "Why you can't be much older than Sylvia."

"Only if you consider twenty years not much."

"I hope this conversation is not too awkward for you," I say, as I take her coat and offer a cup of tea.

"I got rid of my awkwardness a while back," she says. "Tea would be nice."

"Have you ever had Yerba Maté? Good. You'll like it."
Neither of us was there for small talk so while we sipped our tea, I proceed with the topic I wanted her opinion on:

"There are few generalizations about human behavior that stand up under scrutiny," I begin. "No matter what the conclusion drawn from the observation of groups, each member, on closer inspection, escapes the generalization by displaying a characteristic, however small, that is perfectly unique."

I realize that I am sounding professorial. I watch Rock's response to this introduction. Is she bewildered? Already bored? I can't tell as she is looking into her cup of Yerba Maté. I go on:

"The book Sylvia is writing has launched my mind into the world of Personals—their purpose, their efficacy, and especially into the possible psychologies of the characters who employ them. Contrary to my usual avoidance of generalizations, I am going to risk one concerning the size of the penises of men who utilize Personals. I hypothesize that they are more amply endowed than the average."

No verbal response from Rock, but she lifts her eyes from her teacup and observs me with a pained, quizzical expression. Rather intimidating. I continue:

"The reason I have come to that conclusion can be recited by any freshman psychology major: Desire to show off. Meetings with Personals greatly expand the opportunity to display. After all, in nature, birds display, animals display, even insects display in their courting rituals. But with human males, while the craving for praise and admiration, the urge to reveal hidden value, is as strong as in other species, his brilliant tail feathers, so to speak, are concealed. Most other attributes and accomplishments are obvious or easily exhibited—a beautiful face, a melodious singing voice, a graceful walk, a charming demeanor. But here is a part to be admired almost as much as the fetishistic admiration given to the female breast, and it is hidden, secreted, closeted. It is a poem in a drawer, a Helen of Troy under a burka, a Cartier 5-karat in a bank vault. Civilized society is indeed cruel to men with the large ... what do they call it nowadays—package?—Or does that word include testicles?—At any rate, we're enthralled with what you have, society says, but you may not let anyone know you have it."

I stopped. "Well, what do you think?" I couldn't resist the pun, "Have I gone off half cocked?"

"Well, well, well, Professor Alcox, Sylvie didn't warn me. She just said you wanted to talk to me about something related to male anatomy. I sort of suspected you would be fishing for some of my porn literature."

"Oh, no!" I protest, although it had crossed my mind. "Obviously I can't verify my hypothesis in a laboratory, but I was hoping to buttress its credibility with empirical data."

It suddenly struck me that my question implied that she was promiscuous. I am about to disclaim that implication when she answers quite cheerfully, without having taken offense.

"Sorry to disappoint you professor, but my experience in that department isn't extensive. So ... my opinion would be ... what did they call it in my freshman college class—a logical fallacy—generalization from too few samples—I just don't know much more than I've learned from books, movies, and people I've talked to, both men and women. Same as you."

"And your stories?"

"In my stories I just make up anything. The nuttier the better. Your theory says larger than the norm. What do you think the norm is?"

Her question gives me pause. I am uncomfortably aware that my answer would reveal more about myself than I wanted to. "Six to eight inches?" I venture.

"Wow!" Her eyes widen. "More like five to seven, I'd say."

"Yes, of course," I murmur.

Doesn't seem like much of a difference to squabble over, but inches can be important depending on where they're deposited, take Cyrano de Bergerac, for example.

"But I can tell you something that you can factor into your hypothesis, maybe. It's the 'big secret.' Women don't tell it to men because women don't like to make men feel bad about themselves. Especially about something they can't help. But in penises, it's breadth, not length that men should worry about. Have you ever heard a man brag that the circumference of his dick is three inches? No way. With pride they claim a freakish ten inches in length. Pure ego. That's the dimension that sounds impressive, but it's not the one women are interested in. Ask any woman and she'll admit that bulky and short is better than skinny and long. If men would pay attention to female anatomy they'd be convinced. We stretch. Do you know the poet Anne Sexton?"

"Yes. Of course."

"In one of her poems she says she can accommodate an army."

"But that doesn't mean ..."

"Right. Just the same, stretching brings the clitoris forward. Breadth does that. Length only jabs the internal organs."

My meeting with Rock was momentous. She is quite a woman. She would have made a memorable student—like Sylvia—open, inquisitive, audacious, and with an unsubduable spirit, one of those that teachers must occasionally encounter to justify what sometimes feels like a misspent lifetime—the one with pretty plumage as W. B. Yeats said. I would like to engage her in topics other than men's anatomically ambiguous part—the causes of war, for example. I am certain she would not mention such nonsense as the assassination of Archduke Franz Ferdinand of Austria or the brutality of Saddam Hussein.

CHAPTER FORTY-SIX

Ambush at the Village Pump

I COULDN'T DISREGARD the distorted view of Personals my book
might portray. I resolved to respond to the next run-of-the-mill
letter. It soon appeared in my ad-by-author box. I phoned and a
woman answered, although the signature had been a man's name. I
was a little nonplussed, but after all, the man had answered a research
call, not a mating call. I explained myself to the woman and asked
her to relay to Theodore the time and place of the interview and for
him to phone me if it wasn't acceptable.

The face that appeared at the Village Pump entrance was his!
Incredible! It matched the description in his letter, but the
description could have fit a million men who *weren't* Ted—5'10",
thin, dark brown hair, blue eyes, and a feature which wasn't the Ted
of eight years ago: early balding in front, short pony tail in back, "to
compensate" the letter's only cleverness explained. He stood near
the doorway scanning the room for a woman wearing the red and
grey plaid jacket and red tam I had described to the female on the
phone. I felt something like panic, my pulse raced, preparing me
for fight or flight. Escape routes flashed on and off in my mind like
no vacancy signs, but there was no egress but the ingress he guarded,
like a dog of Cerberus. I could remove the red and grey jacket, but
surely the movement would draw his attention to where I was sitting.
I could half slither, half back into the booth on the left and pretend
to be with the couple holding hands and gazing at each other. I
could maneuver my behind onto the empty chair on the right and
pretend to be with the man sitting alone. Even though that would
move me a bit toward and facing the door, I decided to try it, when
Ted spotted me. Our eyes met. I could see his eyes matching my
remembered image with the woman he imagined he would see here

today. I could not remove my glance from his. I saw disbelief and a flash of a panic equal to my own and disappointment and embarrassment. For him, too, it was too late to escape. If only I hadn't glanced at him when he spotted me, he would have had an opportunity to turn and slip out the door. Too late. He walked very slowly toward me, each step planted uneasily, as though the floor was a suspension bridge. Someone had turned this into a silent movie and slowed down the projector. I stood up when he finally arrived at my table. It felt like the stalking scene in a murder mystery. Would neither of us speak? Would we stand just looking, then sit just looking, until a soundless decision was made, and then each rise silently and walk away? Thank god for the small routines that keep the world on center. The cocktail waitress approached, pert in her costume, hugely smiling. "What are you drinking?" she asks. "A gimlet," he orders, inclining his head toward me, "and a martini," as though this were eight years ago and our preferences hadn't budged.

"Well?" he asks.

Was there an edge in his voice? Anger? What did he want me to say? Why should I speak at all?

"Well nothing," I say, hoping the drink would come quickly so that I could hold something in my hand besides my other hand. I notice that my knuckles are as strained and white as if my airplane had plunged into an air pocket. He notices too. The drinks come.

Getting it to my lips would be a feat. The liquid would slip down the front of my blouse on its way from cup to lip.

"Chugalug," he says. "We need two of these." While he looked away to signal the waitress, I manage to down the first.

As the waitress approaches, he gulps his martini.

"Another round, please."

Silence again but the drink has made the silence less tense. I feel as though I could now say something profound or bright or witty. I say, "This is awkward. I had no idea. I never think of you as Theodore."

He says, "I never think of you as an investigative journalist. No more poetry?"

The second drink arrives and I realize that I have absolutely no interest in talking to Ted about the five years that intervened his walking out on me and this moment. I didn't care whether the woman who answered the phone was the one he left me for or another, or whether there were a whole string of women, or how Personals ads came into play. This was simply uncomfortable, and one thing I had learned during the five years is that I did not have to remain in unpleasantly equivocal situations.

"Ted," I say, moving to the edge of my seat, preparing to leave. "I want to thank you very much, truly, for putting yourself out for this interview. But I don't think either of us wants to proceed with it. At least I don't."

"My penalty for walking out on the author?" He says. "You're still carrying a grudge?"

"No. Really, no grudge. I don't interview people I know. I don't want to know what you have been doing. And why would you want to tell me? "

He shrugs. "Why not?"

"Too personal," I say. "Like looking through a keyhole. I hope all is well with you, Ted." I place a twenty on the table and leave. I feel very tough, very decisive, very self-confident.

The pub had begun to fill with Friday Happy Hour patrons. They all looked so eager, so expectant, as though the next two hours would fulfill their dreams. I make my way through the logjam at the doorway.

The evening is very warm. Why had I worn a jacket and hat in July? Protective covering? Some kind of subliminal apprehension about the interview? Seeing Ted upset me with the possibility that I might never find the right relationship. I think of Scott Bigelow, of Boyd Adams. I wished I were with Harry at the deli right now having matzo ball soup and apple strudel, followed by a movie—the Lives of Others. I wonder if Georgie is busy with Randy tonight. I'd give him a call when I got home. Haven't seen him for a while, though I've turned over a number of run-of-the-mills to him; if anyone could get something interesting out of them, Georgie could. If I had turned over this interview to Georgie I would have learned all about Ted's Personals experiences without meeting him. All the way home my thoughts were engaged with the serendipities, coincidences, accidents that move our lives, how inextricably they blend with our choices.

"Who's cooking?" Georgie asks when I invite him over.

"No one." I say. "Let's make it after dinner. I'll pick up a dessert. Book talk. I haven't collected your reports for about three weeks."

"Drab stuff," he says. "But I did have one interview that was quite interesting."

Even humdrum interviews were useful for the statistics they yielded. I'll be able to compare my findings with stats posted on the net. So far it seems that:

1.   When an ad appears for the first time, it brings twice as many responses as when it runs the second time, regardless of the content of the ad. Returns diminish with each successive run.

2.   Men receive five times the number of responses received by women.

3.   Most of the people who answer an ad have answered multiple times in the past.

4.   Most of the people who place ads place no more than three, in total. Why?—It seems that women become discouraged after three attempts produce such paltry results, while men become discouraged when the "right one," isn't discovered among the plethora.

5.   The number of people who formed long lasting relationships with their Personals or who married them is about three out of fifty.

6.   There is only one Boyd.

CHAPTER FORTY-SEVEN

Author Meets Alice

I HAVE TO INVENT a fairly elaborate reason for phoning Alice, yet plausible enough to be accepted by a very intelligent woman.

"This is Sylvia Weisler," I say in response to Alice's "This is she." I hoped her recognition of my name wouldn't require a further identification.

"Oh," she says "the author."

"I hope you don't mind this call," I say. "I'm following up on some interviews—a kind of stage two before launching. I hope (couldn't I find another word for hope?) it's not too great an imposition. Do you think we could get together?"

"What exactly do you want to know?" she asks.

Of course what I wanted to know was how she looked, how her personality matched Georgie's rendition of it, whether she was the kind of heartless person who could dump a lover at the side of the road 1,500 miles from home. I say, "I'm trying to understand why Personals meetings do or do not become relationships, why relationships do or do not last, why people continue to place ads, and why they stop. Maybe the answers are all too obvious, but maybe not."

She laughs. "Did George tell you to call?"

"Absolutely not. In fact he doesn't know that I'm calling and I'd like it to remain that way, if that's all right with you."

"I'm free for an hour or so right now," she says, "If you want to come over."

"Wonderful," I say. "I really appreciate your cooperation."

"My pleasure," she says, with a touch of sarcasm.

We sit in her small enclosed garden on wrought iron chairs at a small wrought iron table. The day is a classical July afternoon.

Brilliant blue and yellow, draped with trees and shrubs in all shades of green, and strewn with purples and pinks. An English garden—romantic, loose and flowing, with untrimmed vines trailing over a brick wall. Not the kind of garden you'd expect of a woman as controlling as the one Georgie described. When a setting doesn't reflect its owner, I wondered, does it mean you have mis-characterized the person? A woman would feel she was lovely in a setting like this, but Alice, in or out of the garden, was indeed as lovely as Georgie had described her. Complex beauty, silver hair, but a complexion as smooth and glowing as a healthy twenty year old's; knowing, experienced eyes, but without a crow's foot or a bag. She was one of those women I had heard described as ageless but had never met.

Within a half hour we had dispensed with all the subjects I had not come to talk about. And during a pause in which I admired the beauty of our surroundings, she adds, "What you don't see are the birds. They love it here, and my favorite, Mourning Doves, incubate and hatch here every spring. They're attracted to flower boxes and I leave the two on my upper balcony sparsely planted for them to nest in." Then she says, "Now do you want to talk about what you really came here to talk about or have you seen enough to resolve something in your mind?"

I don't blush. I often wish I did so that the heat rising to my face would show that I am not as insensitive as my cool demeanor might suggest. My face would have been scarlet now.

"I admit, I've been curious," I say. "I know that you went to PEI together and that he came home alone." I had resolved that I would tell her nothing more, not a word about their trip or when he came home or how he got home.

She looked at me skeptically, knowing that I must know more than I said. Her next remarks were based on the assumption that I knew the whole story.

"You must think I am a ruthless bitch," she says. "Maybe I am. I don't think so. I'll admit to intolerance and cynicism. And I think I've earned them. I used to be a thorough romantic. Can you believe that? Do you know that Mourning Doves are domestic, monogamous birds? Male and female pair unconditionally. There's no such thing as an alpha male Mourning Dove, or a beauty queen female. Did you know they both build the nest and both sit on the eggs until they're hatched, and both keep the fledglings warm and fed?"

"I didn't know," I say.

"But women are not like female Mourning Doves," she says. "We're more like horses. We give men enormous pleasure and we give them comfort and give them power—horse power in more ways than one—and that's why they always want to capture us and own us. In men's eyes we must be broken, tamed, responsive as a push-button. In exchange for allowing this, they feed and water us and provide us with the great loves of our lives—our foals.

"It's better not to have illusions about love," she continues. "Cynicism is built on disillusion. My disillusion grew gradually. Do you want to know what clinched it? It wasn't something that happened in a relationship of my own, or in my marriage, although there was plenty to be cynical about in that mismatch. It was something I witnessed."

Of course I wanted to know.

"A couple of years before my divorce a young couple moved into the house next door. The husband was blind. The woman could almost be called pretty. It was *her* eyes I was most interested in. What kind of eyes chooses to marry a blind man? I liked her eyes. They were blue and alert. Her brows were rather thick and unarched, and slanted slightly upward. Nice eyes. Nicer than most. And she was pleasant and easy to talk to, yet not overly easy; she didn't make an effort to please. For some reason I was happy about that. Her gestures were lively and her expression animated and cheerful, she seemed the kind that whistles when she's cooking. Her name was Anna. I thought what a pity never to have the man who loved you see your eyes and pretty face. The husband was not an adept blind man. He didn't navigate space as I've seen some blind people do, as though guided by sensors. He walked slowly, with a strained expression on his face, and groped the air to avoid hitting something solid. He had been blind since early childhood, but didn't move easily in a world of hard objects. His face relaxed when he was safely seated.

We had spent the evening at the home of another neighbor and a buffet supper was served. "The table is set," our host said. " Please everyone help yourself."

"What can I fix for you, dear?" Anna asked her husband, naming what was on the table. Her voice was kind but casual, without a trace of self-congratulatory selflessness. And this made me happy too. Had I really discovered a pair in which the 'lesser' member did not have to pay for the sufferance of the 'dominant' member? A marriage in which there was no trade off—your beauty for my money, your gregariousness for my costiveness, your social connections for my ears?

During the evening she stroked his shoulder or gave him little hugs. She didn't stay glued to him—and I silently applauded, bravo, bravo—but when she did sit next to him she sat very close. She knew he liked the feel of her physical presence. (Why do couples lose sight of that after a year or two?) And she gave it without embarrassment. Nothing she did seemed self-conscious, as though aware that others were measuring her level of affection or commitment, as, in fact, I was.

Throughout the evening I felt almost breathless, inwardly excited. I felt I was seeing something beautiful and it gave me the impulse to shed my cynicism and try once again in my own life to give all to love.

Later, quite by accident, I glanced into the dining room, where Anna was standing alone, and I was unprepared for what I saw— shocked, almost horrified, actually. Extreme reactions, I know, but it was because of her that I felt I just might recover my belief in love without ego and pretense. What I saw was Anna's face frozen into a grimace. It had turned to stone. And then an almost imperceptible spasm started. It started with a twitch and a tic of the eye muscles and a sudden contortion of the mouth. It traveled down to her arm and shoulder and hip, all of which convulsed and twitched violently, quickly as lightning, and twitched again and stopped. The seizure was over in less than a minute, but I had glimpsed the trade-off. Her husband would never see the distortions of her face and body. In his eyes she was perfect. What must have been to her a humiliating abnormality—was it a form of petite mal—was safely entombed. Most trade-offs aren't visible; they're hidden desires and inferiorities and loathings. So then I concluded for sure that the true representation of love is not Tristan and Isolde. It's Madame O and the Marquis de Sade in drag."

"Now do you understand why I left George on PEI?" she asks.

"I don't know." I say. "But please don't let George know I was here."

"Right," she says.

CHAPTER FORTY-EIGHT

Gathering at Sylvie's Place

I WOKE UP WITH THIS THOUGHT: *Horses used to canter, now they race.* The thought made me feel much older than my upcoming thirty-fourth birthday. My life felt at loose ends, as though the knitter had neglected to weave in the tails of the yarn. I needed to talk to friends who had a way of putting things back in order for me. I would call Harry and Georgie and Rock and Gladwell and invite them over for a throw-together balcony picnic tonight—just appetizer, sand-wiches and dessert. If I was lucky they'd be free.

"Sure, *Medeleh*. What time?

"Sure Sylvie." But I felt as though Georgie could smell my ulterior motive right through the phone.

"Sure, Syl, It will be good to get out. I've been a little under the weather."

"What's wrong, Rock?"

"Eh, who knows? Spleen or pancreas. One of those parts we have inside that no one ever thinks about."

"That would be nice, Sylvia. Whom else have you invited?"

"Just Harry, Georgie, and Rock."

"Good. What time?"

I made guacamole, salsa and sour cream for a nachos dip. Two kinds of sandwiches—avocado, cheddar, Vidalia onion and mayo on thin pumpernickel, and pita with humus, falafel, and tahini with a plate of chopped tomato and cuke to tuck in. For dessert I would serve strawberries and chunks of pineapple to dip into a chaffing dish of melted chocolate. I put on an old Beatles song, "Here Comes the Sun," while preparing the food, and by the time my friends arrived, the racing horses had galloped off. After all, I was only thirty-three at the moment; I was writing a book; a manuscript of my poetry—currently circulating among possible publishers— was bringing encouraging responses; and my financial situation was sufficient to forestall penury. In fact I was one of the lucky ones of the world—the horn of plenty and work I enjoyed.

Gladwell would want tea with dessert. Harry would want coffee, Georgie would want an after dinner drink, and Rock, not sure, but I could supply either beer or a martini.

When your guests are all punctual people, they arrive in a bunch at your door. By the time I answered the knock, Rock had introduced herself to Harry and Georgie and they had all hugged, kissed, shook hands, and were laughing and chattering away, also expressing gratitude to me for relieving them of the onerous chore of providing their own dinner. By the time drinks were served, they were devouring the guacamole and nachos. Except for Rock whose lady-like sips of her beer barely moved a few drops out of her glass.

"Don't like guacamole, Rock?"

"Not that hungry. I'm saving my appetite for the main course."

"It's not truffle-stuffed pheasant, Rock. Just sandwiches."

"Perfect," she says.

My apartment is aligned to the morning sun and afternoon shade. It is mid-summer but a lovely breeze fans my guests, who had filled their plates in the dining room and were now in tête-à-têtes under a mauve sky. Street noise floats up more like distant music than like traffic, and the occasional siren only proved this was Toronto.

After dinner I coax them into the living room so the conversation could be communal, instead of one-on-one. I wanted to talk about the book, at least a little, to my gathering, not just to one person at a time.

Georgie says, "I know you Sylvie. You broke up our lovely repartée to herd us into talking about a *subject*."

"Not at all," I protest. "I just didn't want to miss anything being said at the other end of the balcony."

There followed a simultaneous groan of disbelief and a couple of 'Yeah, rights' and 'Uh huhs.'

"Okay, okay. I want to talk about my book. I've confided my

fears to Gladwell, but they still bother me. What am I doing spending myself—a year or more—writing about game-players, weirdos, hotties, and various flavors of desperation?"

Georgie says, "Well, isn't that what you are trying to find out?"

GA defends my effort with almost the same words I used to defend it to him: "You are writing about what people have done immemorially; they're looking for mates, companions, partners, economic security, excitement, and sex."

Rock: "Romance, too? Love, too?"

Gladwell: "Certainly."

Rock: "Can you really search for those last two? Don't they just happen, like someone sits down next to you on a bar stool?"

"That's what I mean, "I say, although I had already argued out this point with myself. "When you place an ad or answer one, don't you become a product? One says, 'Here's what I want to buy.' And the other says 'That's just what I'm selling'. I've been thinking of answering an ad by saying, 'Dear Seeker, I am answering your ad because I am not what you want ...'"

"Right," Georgie says, "place an ad that says 'Very unattractive, dislikes most things, utterly lacking in charm, dull-witted, ignorant and wants to stay that way, miserly and mean, hates children and travel and any disruption of daily life. Also a sexual predator.'"

Everyone laughs, of course.

"Everyone is laughing because there aren't any people like that," Harry says. "Personals people are just all people. They're all beautiful in their way and they all eat and they all crap. They all do kind and compassionate things and they all do mean and envious things. And they all try to do better. All."

I say, "Or they may be the opposite of sexual predators. They may be sexually unavailable. I interviewed a woman who couldn't bring herself to sleep with any of the men she met."

I notice Rock stiffen as though she was afraid I would talk about Tina. I smile reassurance at her and go on. "This woman said that sometimes she feels as though she could lay every man in the world, indiscriminately, every and each. All those wonderful men out there, with big shoulders and big hands and warm lips. Anyone in pants, as they used to say about 'bad girls' in high school. But when it actually had the possibility of happening, every man changed in front of her eyes. She's dancing with him or sitting across a restaurant table from him and suddenly she sees that his hair grows out of his head in a very specific way, his teeth are crooked, his eyes are small and too close together; she can see the hair follicles where he's shaved. He says dumb things or he doesn't say anything or he doesn't get the joke, or he tells too many jokes. If she were to go to bed with him, she will see the marks from the elastic of his socks etched into his legs. He'll have a hairy chest. He'll have an odor all his own, which she had never smelled before. He'll have a potbelly or a roll around the waist or be skinny or have no calves.

"So there she is, having mentally just dismissed the man who has bought her dinner, she's again scanning all the men in the room. And the next day and the next week she answers ads and the whole process begins again—free floating sexual craving and rejection of each specific man. She has a deep craving for companionship and love, but you can't have those without the other. I don't know why they can't be separated. I really don't. But in this world, love and friendship with the opposite sex inevitably, sooner or later requires sex. Maybe it really is all based on an evolutionary drive to procreate, and maybe hers wasn't strong enough."

Dead silence greets me, as though everyone suspected my example was a disguised confession.

Gladwell breaks the hush by addressing the impersonal observation I had ended with: "I don't think friends inevitably end up sleeping together. In fact, it is extremely rare to leap from a solid friendship into a romantic fire."

"Or vice versa?" I ask.

Silence again

Georgie says, "This is beginning to feel like group therapy, and it's getting late. I gotta go." They all exited en masse the way they'd entered. As he is leaving, Harry says, "See you next week, in boat shoes."

"What?"

"On the cruise."

"Harry, I didn't know you were going."

"You didn't? I knew you were."

"Well, Great!" I say. "See you next week, if not before."

I was stunned. Were they inviting me and Harry as a couple? Couldn't be, since I was 'coupled' with Scott. Blythe had said a crew of two, herself and Barron and four guests. Who was the fourth?

I called Blythe the next day.

"Seems that you and Harry made a couple of conquests at the party," she says. "Scott came alone, and unattached men are rare as deep sea pearls, the most valuable of guests. He expressly asked if you would be on the cruise. And my good friend Penelope was captivated by Harry and asked for him to be invited." Did I care?

"Of course not," I offer the only acceptable response. "It will be great fun."

CHAPTER FORTY-NINE

Boarding a Hatteras Named Windhover

THAT SCOTT PHONED TO SAY he would pick me up at 6:00 a.m. settled any uncertainties about cruise coupledom, yet I still hoped it was not intended for us to share a cabin, which would mean that Harry and whatsername—Penelope—would also share a cabin. I couldn't recall her face. Which one was she among the several who seemed to want to appropriate Harry the night of the fundraiser?

"So early?" I asked

"Boaters start early. Except for the morning after they've got sloshed. But B&B aren't the sloshing kind anyway."

I packed an overnighter with white canvas boat shoes for day (new), yellow boat sandals for evening (new) to go with a sheer cotton dress (new and guaranteed not to wrinkle), its sprinkle of many-colored flowers on a white ground would billow out in whatever breeze prevailed, and from my closet, two pairs of shorts and tank tops and a bathing suit. A reasonable amount I thought. My mind's cruise took place in bright blue sunny weather, but what if it was cold and cloudy? At the second last moment, I threw in a pair of jeans and a windbreaker. And at the last moment I remembered (thank god) that since I slept in the nude, it would be a good idea to pack something to cover myself with in case the head was someplace other than in the cabin. Now my small neat case strained with unsightly bulges.

I was ready when Scott honked, as I'd asked him to do. My sunglasses perched jauntily on top of my head (I had splurged $382 plus tax on Prada—an unconscionable amount for UV lenses in a plastic frame, I thought. It was expensive to hang out with rich friends).

I half hoped Scott would surprise me with an anomalous

automobile—a Ford or a Civic—but, no, he pulled up in an Aston Martin convertible the color of pinot noir.

He hugged me and tossed my case in the back seat.

His legs were tanned, moderately hairy, and he wore no socks. How dumb of me, to have forgot that feet with socks did not go into canvas shoes.

"Blythe tells me this is your first cruise," he says.

"My first on a sailboat," I say. "You'll have to teach me how to stay out of the way of the boom."

He laughs. "And how to avoid the hold, where the slaves are chained to the oars."

B&B were, as always, the most welcoming of hosts. It could not have been learned, I thought again. These were people who were genuinely happy to see their friends.

"Let me show you where your cabin is," Blythe says. "You will be bunking with Penelope. I hope you don't mind. And the boys will be sharing the other cabin. If we were on our boat at the Polo Club, you'd have your own stateroom. I hope you enjoy this cruise. Then maybe you would be willing to join us in Florida for a week off shore."

Both Blythe and Barron had the endearing ability to make their guests feel that they were doing their hosts a favor by allowing themselves to be lavishly entertained.

I was glad to have arrived before Harry and Penelope. This gave me an opportunity to watch them approaching the boat and boarding. They were holding hands, and somehow I found that more intimate than if he'd had his arm around her.

She was lovely. A Viking with fine, silky, pale blonde hair, long slim arms, long slim legs, long midriff, exposed between her halter top and low-rise Bermuda shorts. Of course she wore no socks, and by now, neither did I.

After the greetings, Blythe asks me to show her to our cabin. "It will give you two a chance to become acquainted," she says, "before sleeping together."

"I understand Harry is your publisher," Penelope says.

"Yes. Publisher and friend. This is the third book he's seen me through. The first two were poetry."

"Is writing your work?"

"It's my soul work. I edit other people's writing to keep soul and body together."

Penelope hesitates and says, "I'm writing a book."

Oh, god, I think. Another writer wannabe. "A novel?" I expected her to be working on a formula romance.

"No. It's a study of the first landing on the moon. It's based on my belief that when something happens, it's because all the parts have conspired to come together at a certain time in a certain way. The concatenation isn't observed but it can be traced back, step by regressive step, after the 'accidental' event takes place. Did you ever read the novel *The Bridge at San Luis Rey?*"

"Yes. Long ago."

"Each person and the bridge itself had to move in the same direction, spatially and temporally, for what happened to have happened."

"You're a fatalist?"

"No. Not really. I believe in free will. But I can't help thinking that a complex combination of choices results in what actually happens. Any participant *could* have chosen differently any time along the way. And if they had, something else would have happened."

So, I thought, Harry was on this cruise with a gorgeous heavy weight. And here I was, his swarthy friend writing about Personals advertisements.

"Sounds fascinating." I say.

"In theory," she says. "But it's all in the actual writing, isn't it?"

"I'm afraid so," I say. Why did I put it that way? Didn't it imply that her writing wouldn't measure up?

"Maybe you'll be able to edit me out of mediocrity," she says without sarcasm.

So, I thought, with a pang, a *decent* gorgeous heavyweight.

CHAPTER FIFTY

All Within Reach

THE BOAT WAS ALREADY underway when my cabin mate and I joined the others. We stood at the rail watching the RCYC recede and blend backwards into the waterfront high rises of Toronto.

"It just occurred to me," I say, "that I have no idea where we're going or how long it will take to get there. I just obeyed when you told me to come on Saturday and that you'd return me on Monday night."

"We're heading across the lake up to the St. Lawrence River to Alexandria Bay, New York. That will take about four hours. We'll disembark for a few hours and have dinner, but most of our time for the next two days will be on board. Land is land," Barry says, "but water is a cradle under the stars."

Although she hadn't been on this boat before, Penelope was knowledgeable: "This is about a eighty footer?" she says, "going about seven knots?"

"Eighty-two," Barry says, "going eight. Come on, I'll show you around."

Scott, who had crewed with Barry before, and Blythe, stayed on deck, while Barry showed me and Penelope and Harry the other cabins, the cockpit, where the life preservers were kept, and the life raft. He insisted that we learn how to put the life jackets on and how to lower the raft. Then we met the crew, Paul and Maria Johnson, the latter introduced as the best chef on land or sea in the western hemisphere.

"Before lunch," Barry says, "we'll drop anchor and you can swim off the back of the boat. The water today is calm as a pond. We're heading closer to the shore now."

Before lunch we changed into our bathing suits, and after Barry assured me there were no sharks, stingrays, or blowfish in Lake Ontario, I plunged into the water. I had never swum so far from shore before, and the very thought of it was exhilarating. For a good half hour we frisked and cavorted like exuberant kids, and Harry pinched more 'afts' than anyone else in the game of 'pinch aft,' a slippery version of high school grab ass. Harry played seal by trying to balance a ball on his nose, then he played dolphin by diving with his legs straight up in the air, and then whale by spouting at us.

"Harry," Barry yelled, "You're the best kid of any of us."

"He loves kids," I yelled back. "Maybe that's why." And I thought it would make for interesting conversation at lunch to talk to Harry about his fascination with children, something I've meant to do for years.

I stayed in the water for some time after the others climbed the ladder, which had been unfolded from the side of the boat. Time enough for the skin on my fingers to wrinkle. Just floating on my back, allowing my legs and arms to hang and every muscle to relax, buoyed by the water, effortless, feeling the warmth of the sun on my eyelids. And for the first time in my life I fully realized—I *know* —what life is like for the very rich: for a person to be chauffeured and attended all day, every day, to be able to go wherever they wanted, whenever they wanted, to simply take for their own whatever their eye fell upon, for wanting something to be simultaneous with having it. Before this moment, of course I knew there were some fabulously wealthy people, for whom life was like that. But I didn't really grasp it—the feel of it, the sensation of it. Now I *know* as an epiphany, from the inside out. At this moment, drifting in the silky water, under an azure sky, I *am* one of those people.

"Sylvia, come on up. We miss you," Blythe calls. And I climb back on board, feeling as besotted as if I had been swimming in a lake of gimlets, dry off with a towel that is both crisp and satiny at the same time, and join the others in their before lunch frozen daiquiris. Maria was just leaving the deck, where she had deposited her load of hors d'oeuvres. "Maria, can I help you in the kitchen?, I suddenly call."

Maria looks as startled and frightened as though I had insulted her cooking.

"Of course not!" Barry quickly interjects. "The galley is her canvas. Come and indulge in some of her art work."

"Oh, yes!" I say, striving to recover from my embarrassment.. "They do look scrumptious."

At lunch, Blythe's reference to Harry's childlike playfulness, gives me the perfect opportunity: "He studies them," I say. "You should see the way he looks at kids whenever they enter his line of vision. You'll see if you're ever walking down the street with him and a string of those pre-schoolers pass by, all holding hands and shepherded by a teacher in front and one in back, to protect the would-be stragglers. He actually stops and turns to look at them until they're a half block away. Just watching Harry watch them gives you a vicarious experience of a vicarious experience. You can almost feel how their sweaty little hands feel to each other by looking at Harry."

All faces turn expectantly to Harry. I can see that he is a bit bashful and reticent about responding.

"They make me remember what my body felt like when I was a little kid," he says. "How my hand felt when it was very small, the smell and feel of the sweat around my neck. When I see them walking down the street, I see the scene through their eyes—they must see amorphous confusion, kaleidoscopic images of cars and people rushing by that makes no sense—but just is."

"*I* like children." Penelope pipes up.

I'm certainly not going to say, '*I* like children, too.'

"They always seem to be the best god has to offer," Harry says.

"But Harry," I say, "You don't believe in god."

"Just a figure of speech. I could have said, the best life has to offer."

"If only we could transfer that vision to grownups," Penelope says." If we could see them as expanded children or as children who have just laid down rings of time, like a tree."

Scott says, "But that's exactly the problem. We do lay down rings, layer after layer, each one hardening until the adult tree is a layer of wooden rings. Each layer is more cunning, more self-protective, more egotistical than the one before. No more sapling. No more green and bendable."

"Let's hope so," Barron says. "Bending is what a slave does. He bends down and touches his forehead to the ground. Aren't kids really slaves to us? They *must* do whatever we tell them, even if through love or wisdom we tell them gently and offer reasonable explanations for our commandments. They're still marching orders."

"I think *they* tell *me*," Harry says. "They tell me how to be spontaneous, how to feel happiness in my arms and legs." He turns to Penelope. "Years ago I began to consciously make an effort to see the kid in adults. I take the vulnerability and unselfconscious joy that shows in every movement of a child, and I insert it into a grownup ... the person I'm trying to like at the moment."

Then Maria appears and gleefully summons us to lunch. "My dears," she says. "It is a surprise. You will love it." It is easy to imagine her as a kid.

The swimming and sun and water and lunch have made all of us sleepy, and we retired to our respective bunks for a nap. I drifted off imagining Harry as a father. What kind of father would Scott make, I wondered. Maybe he already was one. I didn't know.

After napping and showering, we gathered in the cockpit where an array of alcoholic and non-alcoholic drinks were set out. We talked a little, not such ponderous subjects as the projection of child qualities into adults, and then each adjourned to a space they select to read or think or just look out through expensive shades at the sparkling water.

Life on a yacht, I thought, just floating along, with everything you want served on a skitter-proof platter and whatever you need just one step beyond arm's length. My sense of what it meant to be extravagantly rich and powerful continued throughout the evening.

After a dinner as magically sumptuous as lunch had been, Scott takes my hand and leads me up to the deck. "There's something I want to show you," he says, and when we are on deck, he points to the sky.

It is a wonder. Only clichés do it justice: the sky is thick with stars. So many that there is scarcely any sky between them, as though a diamond merchant had carelessly emptied a bagful of diamonds on a black velvet pad.

"I haven't seen stars like these since I went camping as a little girl," I whisper. "And even then the tops of the trees covered some of them. I've never seen a whole sky full from horizon to horizon. And, look! There's a shooting one, and another, and another!" I say, "I could be bought with the promise of these stars."

We stand for a while and I am conscious that I must look pretty with the skirt of my flower-strewn dress moving in the breeze. Scott points out Cassiopeia, Sagittarius, the Archer, and Cygnus, the Swan. And I thought, from the placement of just a few stars the ancients constructed an entire action figure. Persons in the sky.

The next day continued much the same as the first, except that we don't swim and, if anything, spend even more time by ourselves with our books and thoughts. I loved it. Solitude amidst company, calm water, and a non-threatening sky.

Blythe asked me if I was enjoying it well enough to consider accompanying them on the boat they kept in Florida. "We're planning a longer voyage," she said, "to Italy. Barron has an office there so we go often. But we try to go by sail every other year."

"Sounds wonderful!" I say. "How long a trip would that be?"

"About eight days on water, each way, plus about five days on land."

"I've never been," I admit, almost embarrassed by my provincialism. Anyone who has traveled anywhere would have been to Italy. "What do you do there? When you go to Italy?"

"Do? Why the same things we do here, but with different people. Oh, I forgot to mention, Barry goes to his office during the day. Everyone else just does whatever they want."

I ask, "What do you do when you go to Japan?"

Blythe gives me a humorous look and backs it up with a laugh. She says, "You're asking if I go to see things like the Sistine Chapel and the Himeji Castle—tourist things? Of course not, any more than I would visit Ground Zero in New York. We saw all the tourist things years ago—the Gardens at Versailles and Duomo Cathedral —the frosting has been dripping off that enormous cement wedding cake for centuries. I'm sure it hasn't changed. When an important exhibit arrives at a museum, Barry usually arranges a private tour after hours, when the building is closed to the public."

We go up on deck, but the sun is small and pale, almost white, as though it had come home late from a drunken party and was still wan and out of sorts. We descend to the cockpit where a lively conversation is going on, and children have been brought up once more.

Penelope is speaking, again on a serious subject: "Does pleasure and enjoyment adapt itself to what is available to be enjoyed? I'm just reading Victor Frankl, and that's what he says about suffering—that it expands to fill the capacity of the vessel—the person's capacity for suffering. Does that apply to enjoyment, or does the capacity for enjoyment contract when there is only a little to enjoy?"

I chime in, "I think that when there is little to enjoy, the great capacity for enjoyment is spent on any little thing."

I am so gratified when Harry agrees with me. "That's one of the reasons I'm crazy about kids," he says. "They can get more pleasure sucking on a cherry Popsicle than Barry gets from his yacht."

"Probably not," Barry protests. "I enjoy my boat, enormously."

"Harry!" I rebut his agreement. "I hate to say this, but your idea could turn into an argument for poverty and deprivation—the less you have, the more you enjoy it."

"I know," he assents. "That's what bothers me about it. But I still think it is true that having too much shrinks our feeling of pleasure. It doesn't intensify or expand it."

"And yet, everyone wants more." Blythe says.

"Yes," Harry says.

CHAPTER FIFTY-ONE

Back on the Ground

MESSAGE MACHINES should blink green for good news and red for bad. I returned from the watery idyll to two very upsetting phone messages. One was from Georgie, and I knew it would have been a red blink from the first word he spoke, ending with a slam eight words later. "Sylvia," he began. He never addresses me as Sylvia. "Sylvia, do not ever call me again. Ever!" Surely this could only mean that Alice had told him about my visit. I phone him and leave a message. "Georgie, *please* call me. Let me explain." Over the next few hours I leave four such messages, and three more over the week. No response. If he was serious it would be a great loss, a great, great loss. Later in the week an envelope arrived with notes about a follow-up interview and a transcription of another.

The second disturbing message was from Tina, *The* Tina whom I knew so much about but had never met. "This is Tina," she says, "Rock's friend." She wanted me to let you know she's in the hospital. Women's General. Nothing serious she said to say. But I believe it is very serious."

I phoned Tina back immediately, skipping all introductions except my name: "What's wrong with Rock?"

"Pancreatic cancer, they think."

"Can I visit her?"

"I'm sure she'd like that."

"Do you think tomorrow, late afternoon? About 5:00?"

"That's when I will be there. I'll see you there."

CHAPTER FIFTY-TWO

Rock at Women's Hospital

WHEN I ARRIVE at the hospital, Tina is already in Rock's room. We introduce ourselves, while Rock gazes at us fondly. The sight of Rock lying in bed, looking exhausted and gasping between words is terribly hard to take. It is difficult not to cry.

"Hey, girl," she says.

"Hi, Rock."

"Could you be my amanuensis? I have important advice for women."

I was always surprised when Rock used an uncommonly big word, though by now I shouldn't have been.

"Sure, Rock," I say, pulling a legal pad out of my laptop case that never holds a laptop.

"It's about posture."

"Posture?" Tina and I look at each other.

"Women are told all the wrong things and I need to set them straight. Forgive the pun. Good posture can change your entire life. It shows how you feel about yourself, and that affects how others think of you. Not *what* they think of you, but *how* they think of you."

I begin taking her dictation.

"For good posture they tell you to throw your chest out and hold your shoulders back.

"Wrong. Like most of the advice you'll get in this life. Throwing your chest forward and pulling your shoulders back yanks your poor body into an unnatural position. It's like bending a dry-cleaner's wire hanger into a different shape."

She speaks very slowly, one word at a time, panting between phrases.

"This is what you're supposed to do for good posture: You let your shoulders *hang*—let your arms drag them straight down, not forward and down or back and down. And don't stick your breasts out like a pouter pigeon. Wherever your breasts are when your shoulders hang naturally and you fill your lungs with air, that's where they are supposed to be, not like they're saluting."

Her speech is labored and she breathes heavily.

"You can tell me later, Rock."

"No. Now!"

"And when you walk, let your hips swing the way they want to. Don't stop the swing or tighten your ass hole. You got that Syl?

"And start right now. You can't change unnatural contortions of the body after forty. It's like trying to unwrinkle an old crumpled love note—it won't lie flat and all the creases show. You gotta start before forty and never quit. That goes for Yoga stretches, too. If you want to be able to bend your legs backward around your face when you're lying down (She winks at me), you'd better start before forty or you'll be stiff as a mummy by fifty."

Tina and I have been sitting still, but I'm sure Tina is taking inventory of her shoulders and chest, just as I am.

Rock stops, her eyes are closed, and I think she's fallen asleep, but her eyelids spring open and she continues.

"Some things you can't prevent. That's the pity. Like your ass falling. Used to be I had a high ass. Now it's flat and saggy and crinkles where it meets my thighs. When you're young you have a flat stomach and a perky ass. When you're older you have a flat ass and a perky stomach. That's the first sign of aging—that ass. The legs are the last to go.

"This is important, Syl. I wish someone had told me this. Open your heart and wag your tail. By the time I learned it, it was so hard to change my body. So hard ..."

She had used up her waking breath and fell asleep.

CHAPTER FIFTY-THREE

Dropping in on Harry

WHEN I LEAVE THE HOSPITAL, the day is just escaping the scorch of an August late afternoon, the blazing sun sliding into the coral light of early evening. Leaves sketch filigree of shadows on the sidewalk, a most delicate and diaphanous lace. I step gingerly, as though my footfall could crunch leaf shadow into dust. The shadows are as beautiful as the leaves, I think. I think the shaded street might be a parable for life and death—the green multitude of leaves, constantly moving, constantly sounding as they move, breathing, like the sea. And the shadows, also in constant movement, in time with the sea, but soundlessly, without dimension, without breath, completely silent.

I have a strong impulse to visit Harry. He's at home and surprised when I appear at his door.

"*Madeleh!* What Zephyr blew you here?" Instead of the usual peck on the check, he presents me with a soft kiss on the lips. "I'm just making something for us to eat."

I smile at his inclusion of me, as though I was expected.

A big pot of water is on the stove and, while waiting for it to boil, Harry makes the sauce.

"Should I make a salad?" I ask.

"Sure. Great. Aren't you coming from the hospital? Why are you looking so happy? Is she better?"

"I don't think so. She's very weak. She dictated to me something about women's posture. I got happy after I left the hospital, during my walk over here: The leaves and the shadows."

"Not the valley of the shadow of death?"

"I wasn't thinking about that. Anyway, I don't think I was. Have you ever noticed that the shadows of leaves are as beautiful as the leaves themselves?"

During dinner I tell him about Georgie's break with me and what I had done to deserve it. "I think Alice is very deep and intelligent. Also she's exactly wrong for him."

Harry doesn't say anything and I am glad he doesn't: He wanted neither to blame Georgie for not returning my calls, nor to condone my action. But he registers the importance of my disclosure by the solemn and doleful expression on his face. Finally he asks, "Did you apologize?"

"I would have if he had given me the chance. I left messages pleading with him to call me. He sent me some interview notes and a tape of what he informed me would be his last interview. I haven't listened to it yet. Do you have time after dinner?"

Georgie's notes say that on Friday he responded to a call from Irwin, the man who suffered from Jewish mother syndrome, but the conversation was mostly a rehash of what he'd said before, and he was displeased that the restaurant Georgie had chosen didn't permit smoking. He was upset that most public places disallow smoking, that smoking had to be added to what people were forced to do in private—farting, picking your nose, masturbating. He was looking for a woman with whom he could openly engage in these activities.

"As to my taped interview, I finally met 'Elegant Blonde,'" Georgie's note says, "if you can call it an interview, you'll see that the woman is not happy. I'm not sure I want to continue doing this," he says. "Could be dangerous. I was expecting her to hit me. I recognized what she said she'd be wearing and as I approached her table, I offered, 'You must be Ruth,' and as I sat down I set the tape recorder on the table and flipped it on.

Harry inserted Georgie's tape into his machine.

"I'm George."

"George? The middle-aged divorced man whose ad I answered?"

"I do apologize. Please let me explain. I am conducting interviews for the author who is writing a book on Personals. She couldn't keep this appointment. I hope you can accept my apology and be willing to tell me something about your experiences in placing or answering Personals ads. You will be contributing to important insights into urban anthropology that ..."

"How dare you! How dare you get me here on false pretenses! How dare you fuck with my mind and my time! This is humiliating!"

"I—I—I'm sorry."

"Women are at the bottom of the food chain. Put that in your book! The top feeders are men—bishops and popes, CEOs, senators. A woman who hoists herself to the top makes headlines—a miracle. Not likely to happen again."

"But I—"

"There are no women at the top. Don't you know that?"

"Well, actually, the author *is* a woman. I—"

"So what? Clitorectomies are done by the women of the tribe. Don't you know that?"

"Yes, I—"

"But on that little conspiratorial atoll where they design the hardware—the automobiles and the armaments—and where they inscribe the outline of governments and religions, there are no women. And do you know why? For the same demeaning disrespect for women you and your author show by manipulating me into this meeting here today. I'm sure you wouldn't have duped a man into meeting you."

"As a matter of fact, I did answer the ad of a man looking for a woman. He was mad too. I ... "

"Go fuck yourself. And pass the message on to your author."

"She was not happy," I say. "And Georgie was probably eager to pass her message on to me. Harry, so far, my book sure doesn't encourage the use of Personals. The stories are so negative, so disappointing, even the good meetings are disappointing."

"Especially the good ones." Harry says.

"Then do you think people might try to find a different way to meet each other?"

"No. It will probably encourage them to use Personals more often."

"That's so perverse. Why doesn't bad evidence stop people? That's what I don't understand."

"Maybe for the same reason women begin correspondences with

murderers in prison. And then marry them. I think people should meet the old fashioned way," he says, chucking me under the chin, "like we did—say, at a poetry reading. How about you and me getting married?"

"Do you snore," I say. "I just can't face spending the rest of my life not sleeping."

CHAPTER FIFTY-FOUR

The Six of Them Again

AFTER GEORGIE ABANDONED my book, I had to be more selective than ever in choosing prospective interviewees. Now to avoid skewing my findings I would have to handle uninteresting responses myself. But I just couldn't bring myself to answer the foolish, the inane, the commonplace, any more than I could plan a second vacation to Toledo, Ohio. After I had visited once, what could I discover in successive trips? Nevertheless, with interviewing, transcribing, reflecting, and writing, I was busy with the book in one-way or another all day every day.

I deserved the day off. I permitted myself to take in response to Penelope's invitation to a day of golf at her club, followed by dinner, capped off by a nightcap at her condo on the lake, for me and Scott, B&B, and Harry. We were becoming a clique. I avoided thinking about me and Scott as a couple, and when I thought about Harry and Penelope, I felt a twinge in the area of my solar plexus.

Rain had been predicted, but the day turned out to be perfectly lovely. It never rains on the picnics of the rich, I thought, and immediately chastised myself for my automatic prejudice.

Blythe and Barry and Harry and Penelope went out for a foursome. I didn't play and Scott insisted on hanging out with me for the three and a half hours it took the others. He gave me a putting lesson—like reading the end of a novel first, he said. And he complimented me on my hand-eye coordination and my ability to avoid using my wrist. Then we played billiards and ping-pong with such ferocity that we were as ready for showers as the golfers when they chugged off the course.

At dinner, the conversation was interesting and easy, as usual, until it shifted to my book.

"It will probably make gobs of money," Blythe says.

Harry and I say in unison, "I doubt it."

"Don't be so pessimistic," Blythe says. "Why not?"

"No violence," Harry says.

"No sex," I say. "At least not of the titillating variety. No movie possibilities."

"But it will be interesting and enlightening," Harry says.

"Well, there are all kinds of talent," Barry says. And for the first time I detected a patronizing note in his voice. "Mine is making money. I began when I was eight years old. I made a contraption of four Popsicle sticks and a rubber band. I sold it to another kid. My markup was 1000%.

"I make the money and my wife (he puts his arm around Blythe) spends it. A perfect symbiosis. I couldn't bear to be married to a frugal conservative egalitarian. That's what my first wife was. A lovely woman. The salt of the earth. But not for me. She deprecated my talent. It was nothing to her. It was as if an artist's wife used his work as firewood. My art is making money. And I love doing it."

From there the conversation slid into dangerous waters, waters in which friendships drown, but I couldn't restrain myself.

"Blythe, don't you ever feel guilty about the sheer glut of your possessions?" As soon as I said it, I was sorry I used the word glut. I could have said "abundance" or even "volume."

"No. Somebody has to have them."

"Has to? Aren't they acquired by sucking up the productivity of everyone lower on the food chain?" Can't I control my mouth? Did I have to say sucking? A simple 'using' would have been confrontational enough.

"You sound like a communist, Sylvia. All right. Not 'has to.' Let me revise that to 'somebody always has,' from time immemorial. Always. Go back as far as you can in history. There are always people like me at the peak of the pyramid and the pyramid always slants down to the vast first tier, the one on the ground. Under that is the netherworld. The shape of the pyramid is the perfect symbol for the economics of the world. It has always been that way and when something has always been that way, it seems justified to say 'has to' be that way."

"So you just ... "

"So I just enjoy the hell out of what I've got. It's all a game, Sylvia, like baseball: there's a whole ground level of Little League. Then a smaller level of Jr. League. Then a smaller level of Bush League, and a smaller level of Minor League. And the top is Major League, and at the peak the players in the World Series. You're playing the game of writing a book about Personals. Barry plays the game of acquiring and manipulating large corporations. He plays in the Major League—the *Fortune* 100. And if he breaks his neck or decides to go wash lepers, someone wise will slide right into his place in the twinkling of an eye."

She said all this in the most cheerful of tones, sprinkled a couple of times with her irresistibly appealing laughter. I said no more, because her argument was sound. I wondered how this friendship could continue between people who would neither lie nor apply the balms of polite deceit.

Scott makes a most welcome suggestion: "I'm ready to top off at Penelope's. How about you?" And we all rose from the table.

On the drive over with Scott, I am glad that he does not ignore the subject dinner had ended with. "You're both right, you know," he says. "Both the implication of your question and Blythe's answer." "I know," I say. "But every day. *Every day* I feel grateful and I feel sad and guilty that I am living in a world where heat and cold don't touch me. I'm never hungry except when my bulging paunch sets me on a self-enforced diet. I have twenty pairs of shoes lined up in my closet, each coordinated with a couple of outfits. Okay, they're not Gucci or Prada, like Blythe's, not even ready-to-wear from Bergdorfs, but they take me to movies and concerts and plays and restaurants. And everyday, *every day,* Scott, I read in the papers or see on the TV people who are starving. Flies are eating the eyes of their children, and people are hobbling on bodies without their limbs that were blown off by landmines or cut off by machetes."

Scott kept nodding and looking sad. He reached over and squeezed my hand, which was lying palm up in my lap.

***

Penelope's condo was stunningly minimalist, with a panoramic view of the lake on one side and the city on the other. From her fourteenth floor it felt as though the building were actually standing in the lake, like a towering yacht under anchor. The camaraderie that seemed in danger at the club eased back into place. We sipped our drinks and talked about Wimbledon and the popularity and talent of Third World authors, my extraordinary competitors. How could a book about Personals vie for readers with an account of escaping a beheading for reading the wrong book, or living as a terrorized minority among a newly liberated majority?

Harry sat with his arm around Penelope. I wondered if he would stay on after we all had left. The thought probably influenced my allowing Scott to lead me out onto the balcony and to fondle me when we kissed.

"Where are the stars we saw on the boat?" I ask.

"They're there," he replies, "behind the city lights. And speaking of stars, I've been thinking about your words on the boat. You said you could be bought with the promise of those stars. I have some connections in publishing and among topflight publicists. If you want to be a star, I could help."

I am surprised and flattered that he remembered and excited by this possibility of literary success, yet I protest: "Oh, but I didn't mean stardom. I didn't mean celebrity. I didn't mean that the stars are emblems of their own brightness—little twinkling egotists. I meant their immensity makes me think of the possibility of the Divine."

"Well, *you* are divine, Sylvia," he says. "Who is Sylvia? What is she, that all our swains commend her?" And I remember that in high school when we read *Two Gentlemen of Verona*, I told myself that I would fall in love with the first man who spoke those words to me.

When we returned to the living room, I find that the conversation had veered from Federer and Asian authors and become very heavy again. Harry was saying (still with his arm around Penelope), that the most compelling reason for marrying was to have someone who cared about you to be witness to your life.

"You are truly alone," he says, "if the only memory that contains your past is your own. The great sorrow of the death of parents," he says, "is partly that the witnesses to your childhood are gone. It's as though your childhood itself has disappeared. I realized that a witness is essential when I gave up God."

CHAPTER FIFTY-FIVE

Dilemmas and Confusions

OFTEN, MY LIFE SEEMS a web of interconnections without a pattern, and I don't feel like I am the one who has woven the web.

Georgie continues to ignore my pleas for a return call.

But amazingly, Kurt Crenshaw does contact me, agreeing to allow me to include his "important" tale in the book. I have an appointment with him this afternoon.

And Blythe phoned with an insistent invitation to fly down to Florida with them and from there to cruise to Italy! "Just three weeks all together," she says. "You must, you simply must! Scott says he will go only if you go! You will have days and days to do nothing but work on your book. It will be such fun! Please say yes!"

"When?" I stammer.

"In September. Just after Labor Day."

And Rock called to tell me that she was scheduled for so many tests that they wanted her to be readmitted to the hospital to facilitate doing them all.

On my way to the interview with Kurt I am aware of people crowding the sidewalks, behind me, ahead of me—throngs. And I wonder as I often do where everyone is going, where everyone is hurrying. And all those cars in the street, rolling past each other, headlights beaming, horns honking. Where are they all going? And in the coffee shop where I'm meeting Kurt, they'll all be leaning across the table talking to each other. What are they all talking about? Everyone has a story to tell, it seems, and wants to tell it. Longs to tell it. Not just for the book. Wherever I am, as soon as someone hears I'm a writer they begin their story. People commit outrageous acts, even crimes for a minute of TV fame. And a book lasts so much longer—"So long as men can breathe or eyes can see, So long lives this, and this gives life to thee." Harry's idea about needing a witness to confirm one's life came to mind and I realized that I was their longed-for observer.

I had arranged the interview on Bay Street so I could drop in at Harry's office afterward, but since I had twenty minutes to kill I decided to stop by now, instead.

"The Addict?" Harry asks.

"Not exactly," I say, still feeling rather ashamed about my weekend with Boyd. "Not the addict you are thinking about anyway. The other addict. His friend from the support group." "I wanted to ask you about something you said at Penelope's, about marrying to acquire a witness. I wanted to hear more."

"Oh. That was when you disappeared on the balcony with Scott. We were talking about having children. I don't think we marry to have children so that our existences can be continued in their DNA. Children aren't good witnesses. They're too vulnerable and you know the lyric, 'Where is the child without complaint.' We need an adult mind, another consciousness who cares, who takes note, who witnesses in the full sense of the term. I didn't say this at Penelope's, but I think the reason for most divorces isn't abuse or falling for someone else. It's that you don't feel that your spouse is paying attention; they're not registering. That's being alone. I think the main cause of divorce is loneliness."

I didn't know what to say. The idea was so like Harry, and it didn't need an answer. So I told him about Blythe's invitation to sail to Italy.

"Are you going?"

"Probably," I say. "It is so grand. When will I ever have a chance at a vacation like that?"

"With friends like B&B," Harry says, "probably often."

I'm no longer early for my appointment and Harry walks out with me. On the sidewalk he says nonchalantly, "Be my witness, Sylvia. Marry me."

"Sure," I say. After my interview. I have to go grocery shopping and have my hair done. Let's see ... It's now 2 a.m. Do you want to make it about fivish?"

"I'm serious," he says. And now he sounds serious.

"Harry!!" I say, "I'm ... what word can I use? I'm flabbergasted. Yes. That's the word, flabbergasted."

"This is not the time to look for the most fitting word. This is the time to speak from the heart. Can't you stop being a writer for a minute?"

"But I am a writer!"

"Is that ALL you are?"

"If you think that is ALL I am, why do you want to marry me?"

"Because I love you."

"Oh, you love me but not the part that is a writer, not the part that is concerned with using the right word."

"You are absolutely exasperating," he says.

"Not as exasperating as you," I say.

Simultaneously we say, "See you later." And we both turn on our heels and walk in opposite directions.

"How's the book coming?" Kurt asks, as soon as the polite greetings are over and we're seated at our table.

"Not bad. How's the dating game?"

"Boring. That's probably why I called you. Kept thinking about the one who got away—or who I pushed away—or who pushed me. Not sure what happened. If you remember I had made up my mind in advance—solemn vow to myself that nothing, *nothing*, would break up my third marriage. And I've kept that vow. I was sure I was immune to falling in love. *Falling!* I never really understood the aptness of that cliché. You *fall*. It's like falling off a cliff. Sudden and steep. It takes your breath away. And it's perilous."

I don't have to prod him to continue. He launches into the story as though he had recently and repeatedly been rehearsing it. I always try to guess what relationship people have to each other when I see a couple in public, in a restaurant or a theater lobby. Are they married or lovers or new acquaintances or buddies; which one is detached and which one is hooked; which one is focused on the other and which one is scanning the room? I wondered what onlookers would make of us—the man talking intently, a monologue. The woman with her eyes fastened on him and silent.

"I met her at the bar of a hotel in Richmond Hill, chosen, since both of us lived downtown, to avoid witnesses to our meeting. I am less careful usually about first meetings. I must have felt that this one would become intimate immediately. It was dark and noisy and the brightest, loudest thing was the TV above the bar. We moved from the bar to a table. It was only 3:00 in the afternoon on a Friday, too early for the after work weekend salvo, even if this bar catered to that crowd. I remember clearly the weather— the air a surprising crackle of cold for so early in October, the flutter of falling leaves, the mellowness of the declining sun. By the time we left it was dark.

"I remember thinking that her looks were neither disappointing nor enthralling, though by the end of our two hours at the bar I was enthralled. If I describe her to you, you won't get it—my enthrallment, I mean. She was nondescript, really, medium height, sandy hair, light brown eyes, evenly distributed features, evenly distributed body."

"That sounds pretty," I say, "not nondescript."

"Well, she did have a heart-breaking smile, but she didn't smile much."

"It was I who had answered her ad. It asked for a response by mail and it was to be written by hand. Now she produced my letter from her purse and began to point out how my handwriting exposed qualities of my character. She said she had almost not answered because my stroke was deep, leaving a considerable impression on the paper, and she was afraid I might be too aggressive, too rough. But the fact that my script was thin had reassured her that I was not a brute. She told me a lot about myself. My rounded letters were evidence of friendliness and my signature, legible and without flourishes, showed that I was honest and not vain. Of course I was captivated, meeting someone, a stranger, whose conversation was about *me*, and who enlisted me in the intriguing job of comparing this stranger's analysis of me with my own concept of myself. She was particularly interested in my tightly closed 'a's and 's's, since this showed a secretive personality; she was married too.

"Our affair began that very evening. It lasted for eight months. We saw each other at least once a week. More when we could get away. What is it that makes one person ineluctable to another person? Is it their mind, their body, their voice, their movement, the slightest turn of head, the way they walk? Is it that they remind you of someone unattainable, like a mother, or some forgotten person who seemed the epitome of desirability, or a movie star, or the first infatuation of your puberty? I searched myself for an explanation of her growing importance to me. Importance is far too tepid a word. I was obsessed. She was on my mind constantly. She inhabited a fixed room in my brain and was there no matter what else I was doing or thinking. But I did nothing with her except go to bed. We hardly talked to each other. We spoke with body and eyes and sounds without words. Like Chimpanzees. Our lovemaking had to contain all forms of expression, all dimensions of feeling. It was insanely intense. Perverse."

His words had been gushing out and he paused now, breathless. I was almost afraid to ask, but his last word lingered in my ear.

"Perverse?" I question.

He continued more slowly, more analytically. "I mean abnormal. We removed ourselves from ordinary, comfortable life. We didn't even think of civility, of politeness. Our world contained no aspirations or ambitions, no wealth, power, fame, duties, obligations, accomplishments, entertainments. It didn't even contain food and drink. After that first day, we never ate or drank when we met."

"This is so strange. You never really knew her," I say. "The real everyday person?"

"No. But is the everyday person the real person? Do we ever know anybody besides ourselves? We know ourselves breath by breath. We feel our hearts beat. We know ourselves by nanoseconds. What do we know about others?—summaries, abstractions, propositions, conclusions. We can never know someone else. But if we love deeply, we can guess at most of it.

"I'm not a religious man, but I've read mystics describe their experience as ineffable and as a disappearance of ego, of self. That's how we were. Anyway, that's how I was. What was important couldn't be spoken. Our passion, my passion, anyway, was ecstasy."

He stopped and I heard myself expelling a great sigh, as though I had just successfully executed a high wire walk.

I couldn't allow him to end the story there. I needed a resolution.

"But you don't see her anymore." I say.

"No. It's been years."

"How did that happen?"

"In a very mundane way. One day she arrived just to tell me that her husband had been transferred and they were moving to the States. Far away. She didn't say where, but I inferred the West Coast. I couldn't have found her if I tried, and I didn't try. Now, I could try to locate her on the Web, but I suspect that I never knew her real name. The name I knew was Rachel. She knew me as Michael. I have always wondered whether my handwriting showed a capacity for obsessive love, which she didn't mention, but wanted to be the object of."

"You continued with your Personals dating, though"

"Not for a while, but eventually, yes, yes, I did."

"Weren't you afraid that it would happen again, or did you want it to?"

"I didn't want it to and I knew it couldn't. It is once in a lifetime or never. I was very unhappy with my life for about a year after that. My poor wife put up with a depressed, inconsiderate man. By the way, it's a story I never told to the support group. Please remember that if you see my friend, Boyd."

"I won't see him," I say.

On the way home, I wondered how my weekend with Boyd had been reported to the support group. Funny, I had never wondered about that before. It gave me an unpleasant feeling. My thoughts circled from there to Harry's proposal ... was it a proposal? ....to a possible voyage to Italy, to Rock's return to the hospital, and circled back again, like a dog sniffing tree trunks, like a monkey jumping from branch to branch. Monkey mind. In the subway station newsstand the cover of Forbes caught my eye. There was my friend

Barry starring at all who passed by as the CEO of B-INC, one of the *Fortune* 100. I was stunned. Not the palatial residence or the yachts had stunned me with the realization that Barry was one of the *machers* of what I was most opposed to in the world. I read the article as soon as I got home.

CHAPTER FIFTY-SIX

The CEO of B-Inc.

IT BECOMES MORE AND MORE incredible to me that a couple of the richest people in the world include me in their circle of close friends. They are warm and available. I could never have imagined that a man in Barry's position would make himself available to someone, even a friend, to be questioned about his worldview. But I had requested and he had obliged and here we were, at his home, in conversation, not related to my book, but simply to satisfy my need to understand his mind.

I search his eyes for an opaque hardness or contempt, but I find only his usual kindliness.

"I myself had been wondering," he says, "how you reconcile what quite obviously are your very liberal ideals with your friendship with us. So I'm glad you called. I welcome the opportunity to tell you what I see as the truth of the way the world works."

"How do *you* reconcile *your* ideals with your friendship with me?" I ask.

"I don't have ideals. Not about the world. I am a practical man, Sylvia. *Realpolitik.* Real economics. Real profit and loss. Whatever ideals I have apply only to individual people. They include honesty, loyalty, generosity, likeability, and intelligence. You satisfy all of those. In addition you are pretty and interesting and my wife is exceptionally fond of you. There is no conflict at all in my feelings of friendship with you. But the same isn't true of you, is it?"

"No," I confess. "There is conflict. I mean all the personal virtues you mention you fulfill perfectly, too. But I think the world can be a better place. So, conflict." How self-congratulatory and righteous I sound.

"Sylvia, my dear, you lead the conversation. Ask me what you would like to know."

I take a deep breath before beginning, knowing I didn't know enough about the workings of economics, world trade, world banks, and so forth, even to ask the right questions. I knew my questions would be too simple-minded, too abstract, too, maybe, unanswerable, but I say, "When I saw your face on the cover of *Forbes*, I must admit, I felt a little surge of pride that such a powerful man was my friend, but I would like to know ... B-Inc is one of the most powerful and lucrative companies on earth, while most of the people on earth are dirty, poor, sick, afraid. Don't you want to do something about that?"

"I do, do something. I give many millions to alleviate the effect of AIDs, to finance pure water projects, to supply food to refugee camps around the world. My list of philanthropies is long."

"But doesn't most of the money you give go to other corporations, to the companies that make AIDs drugs, to gigantic engineering firms that divert rivers and build dams, to huge agribusinesses that grow the food?"

"Well, it doesn't go to them directly, of course, though of course, I understand what you are asking. But corporate power isn't new. It has existed from the beginning, dressed in different costumes and called by different names. There were corporations comprised of kings and their cohorts and their armies—the military-industrial complex of their day. And there were competitive corporations, the 'church,' which had its own armies. In our time, now, the king is B-Inc., the *Fortune* 500, more precisely, the *Fortune* 100."

"And the traditional competitor, the church?"

"In the Western World, it *could* be a problem with people to whom religion is important. It could be as threatening to us as communism was for a short while. In Europe, religion isn't a threat because it's not important enough. In Muslim countries—well that's a different set of circumstances, which I won't go into now, except to say that turmoil, confusion, violence, and war do not jeopardize us. But in America, where everyone has a vote, well, clearly, there are not enough of us to elect one of us. We had to form an alliance with some large group. Unions were out for obvious reasons. The well-educated, upper middle class was out; they're too cynical, skeptical, rational, and they ask why too often. Traditional religionists were out—Jews, Catholics, Lutherans; they've become too tied to the separation of Church and State. We needed a large group whose ideals and everyday lives were steadfastly bound to traditional conventions, to the superiority of the male, the home as the proper place for the female. We needed a group that would be largely satisfied by leaders who went to church on Sunday, continuously talked about the importance of religion in their lives, and connected American patriotism with belief in Jesus. Our genius was the formation of an alliance between the 'priests' of this group and the 'king.' Through this alliance we could not only influence the election of the friends of the corporate system, we could get ourselves elected—even one of us as president of the United States. The brilliant corporate tactic of the century was uniting the 100 with evangelical ministries. Look at their vast audiences, on TV and in the field. That's where our votes come from. In exchange we talk up Jesus, oppose abortion, oppose gay marriage, inveigh against the indecencies, vulgarity, oversexed language of Hollywood. It's a trade deal ridiculously easy and inexpensive. It costs us very little—a few lobbyists. And our victory is compounded; in the very process of buying votes in the marketplace, we sell product."

I am nonplussed that he relates without apology or subterfuge his Machiavellian worldview.

"But you basically know all that, don't you?"

"In general, yes," I say.

"I will tell you more. I may sound like a monster, Sylvie, but I am only a realist. I, we corporations, don't care whether war springs up in one region or another. And as you know, out of my personal pocket I try to ameliorate the suffering of those who are caught in war or poverty or disease. But war is a part of life. It has always been so and it will always be so on this planet. Why shouldn't I profit by the inevitable rather than be one of those who starves? Actually, war is a minor disruption in the grand scheme of things, just as hurricanes are minor disruptions in the life span of the earth.

"How do we respond to the disruption of war? We dampen those that injure the corporation and support those that strengthen the corporation. We're the ones who employ mankind, we supply the jobs, we build, we tear down, we invent. We keep the world working, literally and figuratively."

I become aware of the expression on my face when he comments, "You're more than appalled. You're outraged. I hope that feeling doesn't last. You are my friend and I hope I am yours. Aren't you also outraged by gambling—horse races, casinos, lotteries, ball games? Do you see the people who place bets as evil? Think of corporations as the House at a casino. Everyone bets and some win and some lose. But the House always wins."

I am on the verge of tears. His words seem so reasoned, so true —unvarnished veracity—and no words had ever made me feel so thoroughly helpless. Images flashed in my mind of black children with swollen bellies lying on the ground in Sudan, of children in ads for Christian Children's Fund—adorable kids with huge sad brown eyes and the voiceover saying twenty-four cents a day could save them. What for? All for nothing. All for nothing.

"Then we can change nothing?'

"No. We can change nothing. We can only change our playing field. And the team we want to play on. I want to play with the big forces, the hurricanes. You want to play with the small forces, the books, or even smaller, with the neighborhood newspaper."

"I just can't accept that we can change nothing."

"Not until human nature changes. Then everything will change —automatically—not through political or economic systems— without trying—the way the sun comes up. Can you stop wolves from eating rabbits? You can tame a wolf cub so that you can live with it in relatively little danger, but you cannot stop the wolf from eating a rabbit, until wolf nature changes. And you cannot do that by politics or economic systems. Only the wolf can transform its own nature and when it changes, you couldn't entice it to eat a rabbit. And what would cause it to change its nature is in the hands of ... evolution."

" ... or God."

Barry shrugs.

I don't stay for dinner, and Barry doesn't coax. I carry my

dejection home with me. I remember what Blythe had said: if Barry died, someone would slide smoothly into his slot. Nothing would change. Nothing would change until wolves don't eat rabbits.

CHAPTER FIFTY-SEVEN

Rock's Dying

A MESSAGE FROM TINA on my answering machine says that Rock's tests have become unnecessary. She is dying. Please contact others who may want to say goodbye. I call Harry and Gladwell.

There are seven of us at her bedside that evening. Besides the three of us, Tina and her husband and baby Raquel and Tony.

Rock begins speaking in a thin, faltering, unRocklike voice: "It's my vocal cords," she says. When men get old their cords become thinner and vibrate faster. That makes their pitch high, like a woman. With women the cords get thicker and vibrate less. Makes them sound like a man. With both sexes, cartilage in the larynx gets stiffer and less flexible. Weak voice. No volume. Death does the same thing."

I could hardly stop myself from bursting out crying. Was she going to tell us about the posture of dying too? Then I could hardly stop myself from laughing. She says, "What's with these movie stars pumping their lips full of silicone? Labia lip jobs. If they grew a mustache the two parts would look just alike.

"What a deathbed scene," she says. "A dying Jewish lesbian, a temporary *shikseh* lesbian and her husband and baby, an old fart of an English professor, a writer who doesn't know why she's writing ..." Her voice drifts off and her eyes close. When she opens them, they rest on each of us in turn.

"Sylvia," she says, "I really love you.

"Tina, I love you still and always, no matter where I am. Please remember.

"Raquel," she says to the baby, "Can I pass my godmotherhood on to Sylvia? She'll make a good one.

"Syl," she says, "Do you accept being godmother to Raquel?

"Gladwell, The only reliable pleasure is eating. That's why there are so many fat people."

"Tony," she says, "Tell the guys at the bar that I'd love to write a fucking story about dying, but I'm not up to it.

"Syl," she turns back to me, "Will you stop in at the bar sometime to say hello to Tony?"

Then we all must have blurred into one because Rock fell asleep.

She died that night.

CHAPTER FIFTY-EIGHT

The First Meeting of Tony and Rock

AT THE GRAVEYARD, it was impossible to grasp the reality that Rock's imprudent enthusiasms were confined to such a fine and quiet place where none embrace. When Rock's coffin was lowered into the rectangle in the ground—so isolated and soundproof, so small a space to contain so large a character, Tony broke into wrenching sobs. Men have never been permitted to cry like that. Nowadays it's all right for tears to come to their eyes, even to quietly spill over. But when have we heard men sobbing, their faces contorted and their shoulders heaving? I knew that he was deeply fond of Rock, but this was agony. I learned later that with Rock's death he lost a love that had never been fulfilled. It was the kind of loss that dredges up all the unrealized loves of one's lifetime.

He wept throughout the service. He wept walking to his car.

Was his pain greater or less than losing a loved one to a rival? This is probably better, I thought. It is so *finished*, so free of tormented thoughts about what you might have done differently, what you still might do to rescue the loved one from misplacement in the embrace of someone else.

The day was fittingly bleak and overcast. It had begun to snow—tiny, light flakes swirled in the air like dying moths and were consumed when they reached the ground. The ground became slush and we walked gingerly on the slushy grass and pathways from the gravesite, our shoes muddy and covered with grass clippings.

Tina cried quietly, holding tightly to her husband's hand.

I caught up with Tony as he was getting into his car.

I say, "You shouldn't be alone tonight. Do you want to come over?"

"I won't be alone," he says. "My grandkids are coming to visit and Lily is cooking something special."

"Lily?" I say.

"My wife."

I didn't know he had a wife, and I hoped my face didn't show astonishment.

"I'll come over to the bar sometime this week," I say, "We'll talk."

He nods and leans sideways out of his car door to kiss me, wetting my cheek with his tears.

On Tuesday afternoon I took the TTC to the bar to see how Tony was doing, and find it empty and dismal. An electrical outage had extinguished all the lights and the furnace. I had never realized how cheerful the primary colors of beer and liquor neon signs make a place. One ragged person huddled on a bar stool, no doubt finding even a heatless bar warmer than a doorway. He kept dozing off and jerking awake.

"He won't sit in a booth," Tony says. "Feels it's taking advantage, more than a stool. The bum thinks he's supposed to be uncomfortable."

I worried that talking about Rock would make Tony more sad rather than less. But talking about anything else would be ridiculous. Maybe the subject of their beginning might be pleasantly nostalgic rather than painful.

Hesitantly, I ask, "When did you and Rock meet?"

"Five years ago. I've known her for five years."

I didn't know where to go with this. Maybe he didn't want to talk. I'd ask one more question and if he answered with just a few words again, I'd just drop it.

"How did you meet her? Through your wife?"

"My wife? Hell no! Are you kidding? I met her on New Year's Eve, right here at the bar. You know how noisy it gets here on a Saturday night. Well, triple that. Like a jet taking off. And a crush so tight that all you had to do was turn your head three inches and there was a new face to talk to. Stools and booths completely filled by 6:00 p.m. I had four bartenders who couldn't keep up. People couldn't plow through the crowd to the bar, so the ones in the back or in the booths just told someone in front of them what they wanted and handed them some money and hoped that what came back to them through the crowd was the drink they wanted or some kind of drink, whatever. A hundred partiers talking, screaming, laughing, and singing. Through all that I hear a bang, bang, bang, of someone pounding on a table. Bang, bang, bang, like marching boots. I leave the bar and push my way through to where the banging is coming from. In between the heads and shoulders, I catch glimpses of bright red hair. I think, okay, a drunk, grumpy ole ho who overdid the henna bottle. Tough pushing through those cannibals to the banging booth. Mad as hell when I get there and I look down into the cutest middle-aged face I've ever seen. Bright blue eyes. Skin covered with freckles. The hair was real. She continued banging on the table with a brown hiking boot.

" 'Hey, Irish,' I say. 'Can I help you?' I'm trying to adjust my voice to my unexpected change of attitude. Her voice was 180 degrees lower than what you'd expect to come out of that soft pink mouth and adorable face. Her voice matched the shoe. The rest of her ... what I could see above the booth ... matched the blue eyes and freckles. She looks straight into my eyes and says in a serious voice, 'It's not Irish. It's Yid. And who do I have to fuck to get a beer?'

"It was love at first sight. 'Me,' I say, 'I'll wait on you day and night.'"

"She was something else," I say.

"Yeah," Tony says, "she's something else."
I could see his countenance drift into sorrow and I wanted to break the fall. "When did you find out she was a lesbian?"

"She was no lesbian! I hate that word. Actually Tina came in a couple of years after I met her. Rock was a fixture around here, you know. Everyone knew I was crazy about her. And I provided her with a good market for that terrific porn she wrote."

"Her customers must miss her too," I say, chuckling a little. It seemed too soon to laugh with my usual boisterous laughter.

"Yeah," Tony says, "I'm collecting all the pieces I can find, and I'm going to bind them into a book and call it ... I don't know what to call it. If you can think of a title, let me know."

CHAPTER FIFTY-NINE

Break with B&B

BARRY AGREED TO SEE ME again Sunday morning when I told him that our last conversation had left me troubled in mind. I needed to clarify some things, I said.

When I arrived the sideboard was laid out with Sunday brunch, but I had managed to upset myself past a desire for food, even coffee.

"Blythe will join us in a while," Barry says. "She wanted to give us a chance to talk by ourselves."

"I've thought so much about everything you said the last time we talked," I say. "You seem so sure, so absolute in your analysis about the way the world runs. But many brilliant people disagree with you, people in every field—scientists, economists, political scientists ..."

"Of course," Barry muses. "I often watch these people on panel discussion on TV—intelligent people. There's usually a professor or two, a Muslim, a Jew, a Bush supporter, a Democrat, and so forth, chosen to make the panel seem 'fair.' Each has an opinion to throw into the debate: about the threat of terrorism, the war in Iraq, the environment, illegal immigrants, or whatever. I watch and I laugh. Not sadistically, not in contempt, but in amusement at their inability to get to the bottom issue. Whatever their particular concern is, nobody ever gets to the bottom, and nothing but getting to the bottom will change anything. But that's the way humans have always been—they've always argued and fought about one thing or another that lies in many layers above the bottom."

"That sounds like contempt to me," I say. "And it sounds as though you're patronizing me with your explanation. Why do you think you're the one who sees the bottom, while everyone else is floundering in shallow waters?"

"I like your metaphor. But I wouldn't say 'floundering.' They might know exactly what is going on at the bottom of the shallower waters they themselves are swimming in, but some of them are snorkeling, some are scuba diving, and some even are deep sea diving, but the ones who reach the ocean floor stop participating in panel discussions."

"And you are one of these, I suppose?"

"Yes. I am one of these, Sylvia. I rarely speak to anyone like this. It's pointless. But I like you. I really like you. So does Blythe. And I think ... I hope that you like us."

I nod vigorously. I did like them. Exceedingly.

His quiet laugh is rueful. He says, "In the exchanges between panel participants, intra-country organizations or inter-country wars, it doesn't matter to me who shines in the debate or who comes out the fool, or who loses the war or who comes out victorious. I win regardless of who wins the rhetorical battle or the political battle or the national boundaries battle. I win as long as the debate or the battle continues. My cohorts, the oil companies, also win. Why? Because everyone wants the oil, so it doesn't matter who dominates the land the oil lies under."

"It's impossible," I say, picking up the fading note of our last conversation. "It's impossible in our world that anything, that *anything*, is impervious to change, even the power and profits of oil companies."

"You are right," Barry concedes, "nothing escapes change. But the more things change ...You know the saying. I'm not in oil, but I can use it as a general example of the way things work. There are two changes that scare oil companies: One is that communists take over a country and nationalize the oil. But we effectively have weakened the threat of communism all over the world. Russian communism is a joke. Chinese communism is a joke. The others, Cuba, maybe Venezuela, are too small to worry about. The second is environmentalists—the Nader era of twenty or thirty years ago and now the Gore era. Can you imagine that oil companies will allow alternative fuels?

"Nader environmentalists were reduced to tree huggers and

spotted owl protectionists. And Gore followers are reprimanded for the error of attributing global warming to the paltry interference of human beings. Oil companies will allow alternative fuels when the oil is used up. And by then they'll own the wind."

"You know this, and you can so glibly talk about it? Because of oil, people are being slaughtered. Half the world is on fire and you can talk about it as though you're discussing one of the paintings you are so avid to collect. Barry, I do like you, but I can't have a friend like you. I simply can't." Those words had been in my mind for a long time. Now I blurted them out in exasperation and anger.

"I hope you don't mean that," Barry says gently. "I really don't give a damn about oil companies. If oil weren't an issue, most of the wars that are going on *now* wouldn't be happening, but other wars would be happening, even if windmills were whirling away in every country in the world and geothermal taps penetrated every desert. That is the reality, but it has nothing to do with personal friendships, Sylvie, with you and me and Blythe."

I controlled my tears long enough to say, "Maybe we can't change anything, but we can choose up sides. We can choose. I will miss both of you terribly, but I can't play on your side."

Barry puts his cherubic arm around me. I shrug it off and sit down in the Le Corbusier chair and cry.

Blythe enters the room and seeing me cry, rushes over to comfort me and ask what was wrong.

I say, "I've come to say goodbye."

"Where are you going?"

Barry lifts his hand in a gesture that means don't say anything. He says to Blythe, "I'll tell you later."

Blythe and Barry stand where I leave them, looking after me. I make my way through the three-story foyer to the magnificent front door and a servant lets me out. My thoughts flash back to the first time I entered the home of B&B when Blythe had opened the door to let me in.

CHAPTER SIXTY

A Word with Gladwell

I WANTED TO TALK TO GA. To have him tell me my idealism was silly, romantic, and juvenile. But Barry's views ran counter to beliefs I had held since adulthood—before—since childhood, really. How could I continue my friendship and not see myself as a hypocrite? It seemed like a Faustian accommodation. I opposed NAFTA, the power of the World Bank, the ever-widening gap between the Middle Class and the rich. But at the same time I was enjoying the affections of people who were the very instruments of all these things, and accepting the luxuries provided by everything I hated.

My conscience urged me to terminate the friendship. My heart didn't know if it could tolerate another loss. Rock gone. Georgie gone. I needed to talk to GA.

His message machine said he was at a conference of the Modern Language Association in New York and offered the number of his hotel—for emergencies, I'm sure, not for using his ear to spill my emotional conflicts into. But I telephoned anyway, and that evening he returned my call. He said, "Sylvia, you knew their work and their position in society from the beginning."

"I didn't know he was in armaments manufacturing."

"What is the difference—armaments, drugs, oil, shipping ...?"

"I knew they weren't 'Society': not old money. They were from the middle class ... my class."

"Someone may rise to the top of the pyramid even from the working class, for that matter, that doesn't change the structure of society. The individual inserts himself into the old structure, which easily, even happily welcomes a newcomer to occupy the seat occupied by one of their own who died or skidded downward. In fact that rare ascendant person protects the top, makes it seem so attainable. It reifies the American Dream.

"Sylvia, dear, I can't help you. In a way I admire your decision. In a way I think it is foolish. It will change nothing."

I was startled when GA used words identical with Barry's.

"It will change me," I say.

"Yes, my dear," he says. "Sleep well."

But I couldn't sleep well. I called Harry.

"Hi, Syl," Harry says. "What's up?"

"Nothing. I just need someone to talk to."

"Problem?"

"Not exactly. Confusion."

"Can it wait until tomorrow. I have a friend visiting." Pause. "Penelope. Want to say hello?"

"Not in the mood," I force myself to say lightly. "I'll talk to you tomorrow."

Penelope in Harry's apartment did nothing to quell my distress. How ironic. Just as I was terminating my involvement with my rich friends, Harry was cementing his with a rich female friend of my rich friends, the beautiful, brainy Penelope. *Sleep well. Right.*

Harry called at 8:00 in the morning. "Did I wake you?"

"Didn't sleep."

"What's the matter?"

"The sound bite version is that I ended my friendship with Blythe and Barron."

"Did you have an argument?"

"Didn't argue. Not at all. I just went over there and said good-bye."

"For god's sake, why?"

"Because they're on the wrong side."

There was a long silence while I know Harry was trying to fit this statement into different slots in his brain. Being Harry, I knew he would find the right one.

"Why don't you come over," he says.

CHAPTER SIXTY-ONE

The End of One Personal Story

HARRY'S REACTION to my reasons for, and account of the breakup with Blythe and Barron is unexpected. His immediate response, though, is a question:

"Did you break off with Scott Bigelow too?"

The question takes me aback. "Scott? No, I didn't. That never occurred to me. Is he so rich?"

Harry looks at me quizzically. "Very. Rich as Croesus or, I should say, Midas. He can touch a garbage dump and turn it to gold. In fact, I think industrial waste disposal is one of his enterprises. But he is best known for manufacturing paper."

"Oh," I say, "*that* Bigelow."

With that Harry puts his arms around me, looks into my eyes (His are hazel with little yellow specks.) and says, "For the third time, will you marry me?"

"I didn't think you were serious the first two. Harry, you don't even think I'm sexy."

"Sylvia! You sometimes can be so sure and so wrong. It makes me worry about the observations in your book. I think you're the sexiest woman I've ever known."

"My observations are exquisitely accurate!"

"Then I worry about your power of intuition. I've been in love with you for three years. Couldn't you see it, feel it, sense it?"

"At the beginning I thought so. Then we just seemed to sink into a solid friendship."

"It's that too ..."

"I can't give you my answer until you tell me how you love me. Count the ways, Harry."

His voice drops to a low, soft octave, almost crooning and his hands caress me, running over my face and shoulders and breasts and waist and hips. He says, "I love every sexy part of you and the way all the parts are put together."

"Okay" I say. "That's one."

"I love you because sometimes you are not smiling, sometimes you don't need to be charming, sometimes you don't need either to please or confront. I find that incredibly sexy."

"That's two."

"I love you because there is no one else I want to watch me making love. And no one else I want to watch making love to me. I don't want anyone else to watch you. I want to be the only witness.

"I want to marry you because I want to have your eyes on my life and your hands on my life. I want to share the journey of your pilgrim soul."

I can't speak.

He says, "You're the author. You can break my heart and turn this into a tragedy, or you can marry me and turn it into a comedy."

I pushed off from his chest and looked into his face. "A comedy?"

"Yeah," he says, "as in Shakespeare's comedies. In the tragedies the lovers die. In the comedies they get married—they're the glue that holds the world together."

I replace myself against his body and nod my head vigorously. "Yes," I whisper, "I will." And then I resume kissing where my lips reach, his neck and the underside of his chin.

Later, I say, "But I'm worried. I've interviewed all those men who love variety. It looks like nature intended it—look at the bees and the flowers."

Harry says, "Look at Monet and the water lilies."

"I'm worried, too," he says. "How will you feel when I take off my pants and you see sock indentations on my calves?"

"I won't mind," I say. "I won't mind even if you get hair on your back that ends in a tail."

Gladwell Alcox Provides an Endword

THE WEDDING OF SYLVIA WEISLER and Harry Sympler did not appear in the pages of *Vanity Fair* nor even in the columns of *Toronto Life*. Had the guest list included the CEO and wife of B-Inc., the wedding would have superimposed at least a two by three candid upon the glossy displays of coutured women hanging on the arms of tuxedoed men. Harry has an extensive *mishpucha*, so the wedding was a large one. Sylvia's family is minute, so, she said, she extended it with her favorite people, which included Tony, Tina with her husband and Georgie. It was not within the capability of Georgie's capacious heart to continue to refuse Sylvie's contrition when one of her abject apologies arrived with a wedding invitation. I gave the bride away and hope one day to become Uncle Gladwell.

Good Reader, I trust you kept your wits about you throughout the reading of the first draft of this book. You knew long before she did that Harry was in love with her. And you knew that my continual prodding of her motives was aimed at bringing her to acknowledge that her quest was personal, not societal. It took her a while to find that, as in Anderson Fairy Tales, she already possessed what she was looking for.

Nevertheless, *The Problem with Personals*, slated for spring release, is not an unimportant testament to the disintegration of our social norms. The manner in which we search for love and mates is not merely an alteration of taste or manners or political or economic realities of our time. Over the past one hundred years, the major power structures of society have remained the same. But personal social structures have changed enormously, especially as regards the family and the way in which one does or does not go about achieving one. Marriage has always been the primary fixative of a stable society, and marriage is happening increasingly late and less frequently.

I look forward with interest to the next subject Sylvia will investigate—despite her publisher husband, she will run whatever she writes past me. Perhaps a book on the importance to children of unrelated 'uncles.'

The two are on their honeymoon now. The last words I heard from them, I overheard. Sylvie was quoting Robert Frost "Nothing done to evil. No important battle won." Harry's reply was almost inaudible, but I think he said, "But it's better than the other way."

Acknowledgements

I want to thank Andrew Steinmetz, my editor, for once again helping me over obstacles and guiding me around patches of black ice.

I want to thank my friends Sherry Gluck, Marcia Shinkaruk, Hope Guam, and Chris Theroux for their comments on various passages of the raw manuscript, while it was still pliable.

I want to thank, especially, my friend and colleague Beverly Ricks, who read the penultimate version cover to cover, and offered her "first reader" responses for every single chapter.

I want to thank all those authors, living and dead, whose unforgettable words are sprinkled so liberally throughout this book.

As always, there are far more people that deserve thanks for the production of a book than it is possible to name.

ESPLANADE
Books

THE FICTION SERIES AT VÉHICULE PRESS

[Andrew Steinmetz, editor]

A House by the Sea : A novel by Sikeena Karmali

A Short Journey by Car : Stories by Liam Durcan

Seventeen Tomatoes : *Tales from Kashmir* : Stories by Jaspreet Singh

Garbage Head : A novel by Christopher Willard

The Rent Collector : A novel by B. Glen Rotchin

Dead Man's Float : A novel by Nicholas Maes

Optique : Stories by Clayton Bailey

Out of Cleveland : Stories by Lolette Kuby

Pardon Our Monsters : Stories by Andrew Hood

Chef : A novel by Jaspreet Singh

Orfeo : A novel by Hans-Jürgen Greif
[Translated by Fred A. Reed]

Anna's Shadow : A novel by David Manicom

Sundre : A novel by Christopher Willard

Animals : A novel by Don LePan

Writing Personals : A novel by Lolette Kuby

Véhicule Press
www.vehiculepress.com